HEARTBREAKERS

HEARTBREAKERS

They're the rockers every girl wants and every man craves to be: talented, good-looking, wildly successful, and with money to burn. The band Mesquite is all these things and more. But success comes with its own price. Everyone wants a piece of the Tristan brothers. Brian, Paul, Caz, and Nick stick tight to guard themselves from the vagaries of the world. Who better to sneak under their defenses than four little heartbreakers made just for them?

Previously available only in electronic format, these steamy novellas and short stories have now been combined for a paperback edition!

Included are the tales…

What About Love?
Crazy On You
If Looks Could Kill
Magic Man

PRAISE FOR CAITLYN WILLOWS

WHAT ABOUT LOVE?

"5 Blue Ribbons!...Caitlyn Willows really drew out all my emotional hotspots with *What About Love?* In a matter of moments I was drawn into this storyline and found myself experiencing anger, hurt, tears, and even adoration right along with the characters. I'd love to say I want Brian for myself but he and Lexy are so perfect together that I couldn't imagine even trying to tear this couple apart. This story is sexually charged and intense as well as endearing—all the things I've come to appreciate in Ms. Willows's storylines. Ms. Willows does a beautiful job capturing the essence of this musical group as a whole but also allows readers to see each [member] as very different individuals. Fortunately readers can get to meet each of the characters up close and personal through the other stories in the *Heartbreakers* series."

—Chrissy Dionne
Romance Junkies

CRAZY ON YOU

"5 Blue Ribbons!...*Crazy On You* is the second book in Caitlyn Willows' *Heartbreakers* series and I thoroughly enjoyed this story. With today's paparazzi it's easy to understand just how quickly rumors and lives can spiral out of control, but these brothers seem to be very down to earth and devoted—not just to each other but their loved ones and fans as well. I found these characters to be charming, realistic and lovable but also refreshingly vulnerable. Ceci and Paul complement each other beautifully and even though they're both typically 'vanilla' or 'Mr. Missionary,' as Paul's brother, Caz likes to tease Paul, it's obvious that with the right incentive and opportunity anyone is capable of enjoying a little 'kink' in their love life."

—Chrissy Dionne
Romance Junkies

If Looks Could Kill

"5 Blue Ribbons!...*If Looks Could Kill* is the third story in Caitlyn Willows' *Heartbreakers* series and it's definitely a hot read that will incite readers to pick up copies of the other books in the series. The tension between Caz and Brooke is captivating right off the bat and plays out in ways that leave you envious—especially once they're forced to confront their desires and able to be true to themselves. This is a wonderful addition to the *Heartbreakers* series and if you haven't had the opportunity yet, I'd suggest picking up the other books in this series."

—Chrissy Dionne
Romance Junkies

Magic Man

"5 Blue Ribbons!...With *Magic Man* we're treated to Nick and Gaby's tale and all the tension and wonder that goes along with it. Not to mention a bit of humor that had me chuckling over the thoughts that run through Nick's mind. Gaby's a tough cookie but with Nick she seems softer and vulnerable—maybe not a true submissive but perfect for him just the same. What I truly got a kick out of is Gaby's father's attitude. He's a softie when it comes to her but there's no doubt he instills a healthy amount of respect from everyone around him. These characters [in the entire series] have charmed their way into my heart with their down-to-earth personalities and lack of 'rock star ego.' Caitlyn Willows successfully brings these men and their storylines to life so the reader feels like they could really be a friend and not just idols standing on a stage belting out favorite tunes."

—Chrissy Dionne
Romance Junkies

Also By Caitlyn Willows

All Four One
Bend Me, Shape Me
The Boys Are Back
Caitlyn's Kisses, Vols. I-V
A Corner Of My Soul
Forbidden Fruit
Graduation Day
The Heartbreakers Series (Books I-IV)
Her Bounty
Hired Hand
Hotel California
Just Partners
Love Potion #9
Lust Letters
Midnight Rendezvous
One To Grow On
One Touch
Our One True Love
Playtime
Showtime
The Star Series, Books I-V
Tainted Love
Teamwork
Thief Of Hearts
Treasure Hunters
Undercover Lover
White Lies

HEARTBREAKERS

BY

CAITLYN WILLOWS

AMBER QUILL PRESS, LLC
http://www.amberquill.com

HEARTBREAKERS
AN AMBER QUILL PRESS BOOK

Amber Quill Press, LLC
http://www.AmberQuill.com
http://www.AmberHeat.com
http://www.AmberAllure.com

ISBN 978-1-60272-893-6

Layout and Formatting provided by: Elemental Alchemy

PUBLISHED IN THE UNITED STATES OF AMERICA

Table Of Contents

WHAT ABOUT LOVE

CHAPTER 1

Brian Tristan locked his attention forward and forced himself to maintain the precise speed limit. Paparazzi trailed him, as they always did since Mesquite had hit the big time. At first it'd been cool to be the focus of attention, but as the years rolled by it had grown old fast. Now it was all he could do to stay polite. Keeping a public face on twenty-four/seven sucked. The situation was only growing worse.

He and his brothers couldn't take a shit without the media wanting to tell the world about it. The temptation to slam on his brakes and throw a little panic into those hugging his tailgate was almost too much to bear. Someone needed to pay for the agony twisting his guts; it might as well be one of the paparazzi.

Not once during their long climb up the ladder of success did the Tristan brothers ever imagine that heaven and hell could be so intricately entwined. They'd wanted to write their songs and share them with the world. Somewhere in that desire their dreams came true. They were wealthy beyond their wildest imaginations, and too damn busy to take full advantage of it. Too much it the public eye to really have a life. But they'd all agreed to ride the crest of this wave as long as they could. Heaven was the money and the fans. Hell was the news media that hounded them all, Brian more so than the others. Because Brian had made the mistake of dating Ceci Powers, and the world wanted to know every little detail.

"Either marry her or end it now!"

Paul's shout still echoed through his head. Brian had never seen his brother so upset. Like he had a personal stake in Brian's ongoing relationship with Ceci.

Well, he supposed Paul did. So did Caz and Nick. Ceci had been a constant fixture in their lives since he'd met her a year ago. Marrying her would just make her officially related, rather than a pseudo-sister to his brothers. Ceci was great fun, beautiful, smart, had a great laugh. His brothers loved her. His *parents* loved her. The only problem was...Brian didn't.

Oh, he liked her well enough. The sex was good, although he couldn't remember the last time they'd had any. Some time before Mesquite's latest tour. Or had it been longer than that? Caz told Brian he was suffering from cold feet because of the family's pressure to pop the question. Having misgivings was a possibility because Brian wasn't exactly ready to make that move, but he also hated the idea of never seeing Ceci again, never having her as part of their lives. Hence Paul's ultimatum.

Mesquite had finished up their tour the week before. Though Brian had seen Ceci, it seemed he'd done everything in his power to avoid being alone with her. They hadn't even shared a kiss, much less a bed. To her credit, Ceci didn't push him for private time. Paul was right—it wasn't fair to keep her dangling, for lack of a better word. The idea of ending it tortured his conscience. Like the family, Brian really liked her. But love? No, there was only one woman he'd ever love—the one he let go all those years ago.

Not a day went by that Brian didn't regret the choice he and Lexy Claremont had made. It was for the best, they'd said. Each had different goals. It was crazy to be so in love with just a glance. They thought that meant it had to be sexual attraction and nothing more than crazy hormones at work, certainly not something meant to last. But it was. Brian's heart knew it, his body knew it, his head... still argued. Every love song he'd ever written was for Lexy. Every note that flowed from his voice was for her. How many times had he thought of calling, of showing up on her doorstep with his heart in his hand? And each time he talked himself out of it. What if she didn't love him back? What if it all was just a crazy, crazy fling? Wasn't it better to remember that weekend as supreme rather than spoil the memory with a confrontation now? His heart wouldn't be able to take knowing Lexy really didn't care and never had, that he was only a weekend fuck.

Others had substituted for Lexy in his bed, Ceci the most recent. But as much as he tried, Brian didn't love Ceci. It wasn't fair to her to stay together, was it?

Somewhere in the emotional turmoil crowding his head and churning his gut, Brian realized they needed to talk. Perhaps they could salvage a friendship from the ashes of their affair. He'd wanted to talk to her privately. It was Ceci who'd suggested they meet at their favorite restaurant for a quiet dinner. He owed her that much. Afterward, they'd go back to her place and… The thought of hurting her churned his gut all the more.

The red neon sign for Prestige caught his attention the instant Brian turned onto the crowded Malibu street. The restaurant was still a block away, but those big block letters sliced the night like a lighthouse beacon. Perched overlooking the Pacific Ocean, it was probably just that to some sailors.

He gripped the steering wheel, hoping his sweating palms wouldn't execute a U-turn and head for home. That would make fodder for the tabloids. He could see it now.

ROCK STAR BAILS ON GIRLFRIEND!
CECI IN TEARS!

They'd run old photos, doctoring them to make it look like Ceci was crying. If she wasn't humiliated before, she would be once the media got done with them both.

Brian pulled in a breath and aimed for valet parking at Prestige's entrance. He hated having a stranger in his Cherokee, hated the extra invasion of his privacy. And he sure as hell could never leave anything personal in the vehicle. They'd learned that mistake early in their careers when fans rifled through their cars for personal items to keep or sell on eBay. But Prestige played by its own rules—*they should have named it "Pretentious."* If you wanted to eat here, your vehicle would be attended by a valet. That meant going over everything inside to make sure nothing was left to pilfer or snoop at.

Plastering on his public smile, Brian eased his vehicle to a stop. A valet, who looked barely old enough to drive, dashed up. Bright eyes widened when he spied Brian. In the few seconds it took Brian to exit the vehicle, the valet had turned into a quivering mass of adulation. Images of gouges and dents on his black beauty scoured Brian's head.

"I'll…I'll take good care of her, Mr. Tristan," he stuttered.

"I have no doubt." He clapped the young man on the shoulder and headed for the entrance.

Thick red carpet cushioned his footsteps. Camera flashes haunted his every move. Too bad the owners couldn't have extended the effort to ensure the privacy of its patrons. Brian practiced polite indifference when it came to the paparazzi, no matter how violated their presence made him feel. Lifting a wave, the semblance of a smile, posing on occasion kept everyone happy, more or less.

For all its outward appearances, Prestige left snobbery at the door. The food was great, but pricey. The waitstaff friendly and accommodating, eager to please. And California casual attire was more than welcome— not too casual… swimsuits and flip-flops were still out. Jeans were frowned upon, unless they were molded to the ass of a hot chick working her way to the A-list. Brian stuck to trousers and a long-sleeved shirt to cut the chill blowing in off the ocean. Ceci, a reluctant slave to the fashion goddess, always chose to freeze in a short, sleeveless dress that showed off her great legs and pebbled her nipples.

Talk about a photo op.

The doorman swung the door open two steps before Brian reached it. "'Evening, Mr. Tristan."

"Good evening." He smiled and slipped the man a hefty tip as he shook his hand. The pass-off was smoothly executed.

Inside, the maitre d' was just as quick. "Welcome back, Mr. Tristan. Ms. Powers arrived a short while ago and requested to be seated."

"Excellent." Another tip.

"Thank you, sir." The man snapped up two menus and swept his arm before him. "This way, sir."

Brian followed him into the crowded dining room. Candle globes looked like miniature campfires at white-clothed tables, illuminating the faces of people leaning close in hushed conversation. No one looked his way. The west wall facing the Pacific Ocean was all windows. Dressed in an azure shift and high-heeled sandals, Ceci gazed out the window, elbow on the table, chin perched on the tips of her long, red nails—nails that had caught his attention from the start because they reminded him so much of Lexy's. He shivered at the memory of how they'd felt raking down his back, an action no other woman had ever been able to reproduce.

Ceci's glass of white wine remained untouched before her. Sun-kissed brown hair drifted in long waves down her back. She looked sad, troubled. Guilt weighed Brian down. She was just so damned nice.

Her gaze shifted from the view to Brian's reflection. Smiling, she turned to face him. "Hi."

"Hi." He leaned down to kiss the cheek she offered to him, then slid into his chair.

The maitre d' parked the menus in front of them, then gave them privacy. Outside, the cameras still lingered. He could see light reflected from the lenses.

"Been waiting long?" Brian picked up the menu, but didn't bother to look at it.

"Not long at all." Ceci perused the selections, then set her menu aside. "Brian, about this week..."

"I know." He dropped his hand over hers and played his thumb over her knuckles. "I have no good excuse. I think..."

A waiter suddenly appeared beside the table, so quickly Brian wondered if he'd been transported in. Chilled champagne nested in a sterling silver bucket of ice. Crystal flutes gleamed in the candlelight. With a broad smile, the buck-toothed waiter set the glassware in front of them. That's when Brian noticed the gold ribbon cascading from Ceci's glass. A notecard was attached to one end.

Ceci plucked the ribbon up. A diamond ring dangled from the other end. Her eyebrows edged closer in a puzzled expression Brian was sure matched his own. She flipped open the card with her thumb, then glanced up at him, eyes wide.

"Marry you? You're asking me to marry you?"

Brian's mouth fell open, punctuated by the muffled pop of the champagne cork. *If this is Paul's idea of forcing the issue—* The maitre d' rushed the table amid a flurry of camera flashes going off outside.

"My sincere apologies, Mr. Tristan...Ms. Powers." He grabbed the waiter's arm and hissed, "You got the wrong table."

Nearby, a man tossed his wadded napkin to the table. Obviously *he* was the prospective groom and the woman, whose face wavered between joy and upset, was his intended bride. More cameras flashed, recording every humiliating second as the maitre d' removed the surprise and tried to do damage control.

Brian managed to recover his heartbeat and looked at Ceci. She stared at the table, shaking hands folded on the table. God only knew what she was thinking, what the media was going to say about all this. He liked Ceci...a lot. He didn't want her out of their lives and couldn't bear to think of the pain she must be going through at that moment. Paul was right. It was time to shit or get off the pot.

He covered his hands over hers, pulling her fingers into his. "Let's do it." He ducked his head, trying to catch her gaze.

Slowly her sea green eyes lifted to him. "Wh-what?"

"Let's do it." He added a smile. "Let's get married."

"Oh…o-okay." She nodded. "S-sure. Y-yes."

As if by afterthought they leaned over the table and kissed to seal the deal. More flashes assaulted them.

Brian eased back and signaled the maitre d' with a lift of his hand. Instantly the man was by their side.

"We'll take that bottle of champagne after all. Looks like Ms. Powers and I have a little celebrating of our own to do. And put the other lucky couple's bill on mine."

CHAPTER 2

"You asked Ceci to marry you?"

Brian hated when Paul hovered over him like this. It always made him feel inadequate, subservient…stupid, which was why Paul did it.

He frowned and shoved to his feet, matching his brother's six-foot height. Paul's dark-eyed glower didn't fade. "Yes, sort of."

"Sort of?"

God, Paul looked like their dad right now. The resemblance unsettled Brian all the more.

"Either you did or you didn't? Which is it?"

Yep, just like their dad.

"I did," he snapped. "What are you so pissed about? Quit interrogating me. It was your idea." He briefly explained the circumstances behind the proposal. The information didn't ease Paul's anger.

"So you're telling me that you proposed because you didn't want Ceci out of your life?"

"Well…yeah." He shrugged. "I like her."

Paul's face reddened. "Like her? You *like* her?" he exploded.

Brian jerked from the impact and took a step back.

Fists at his sides, Paul covered the short distance, shoving his face inches from Brian's. "You *like* her? What the fuck, Brian. What about love?"

Brian struggled for a response. Instead, he got defensive and shoved Paul away. "Leave me the fuck alone. I thought you'd be pleased. This was your idea."

"That's just it, Brian. It should have been *your* idea."

"I'll take that to mean you don't want to be the best man." It was the best comeback Brian had because, in his heart, he knew Paul was right.

"Oh, I'll be there. Right by your side. Ceci deserves to have at least one man at the altar who loves her." He executed a crisp about-face and strode from the room. Obviously they wouldn't be working on new songs today.

Brian sank into his chair, rested his elbows on his knees, and buried his face in his hands. As much as he hated to admit it, he needed a little away time from his brothers. In hindsight, buying a house together wasn't such a great idea. Their parents had told them they were crazy to do it. *Looks like they were right.* He really needed his own space. They'd bought this house for convenience sake at the time. Every waking hour was spent in the recording studio out back, writing new songs, or being on tour. They were rich and successful beyond their wildest imaginations. The pressure was starting to take its toll.

He heard footsteps squish across the carpet, but didn't move until he saw three sets of feet before him. Paul, Caz, and Nick all ganging up on him?

"What?" he asked without looking up.

"Is there something you want to tell us?" Caz asked.

"Any unfinished business perhaps?" Nick added.

"I don't know what you mean and I don't feel like playing games with you guys," he mumbled through his fingers.

The front door slamming echoed through the cavernous house like a gunshot. High heels clicked over the ceramic tile on a direct path to their den. Brian swore he could even hear them stab into the carpet pile once the visitor hit that area. Only one woman had open access to their house. This was one argument Brian didn't want Ceci to walk in to. Before she could reach the room, the doorbell chimed. They monitored her progress to the front door and back, this time with less force in her stride and the squeak of rubber soles in time with hers.

One by one the brothers sat in their respective chairs, leaving no open places to sit. Caz used the worn coffee table as a footstool, crossed his ankles, and leaned back like he was ready to watch a movie. The only thing missing was the popcorn and beer. God, how long had it been since they all kicked back like that?

Their manager, Howard Ramsey, crossed the threshold first. His fingers worried what little hair he had left, alternately mussing and then smoothing the black strands. Ceci stepped in behind him, face tight with no trace of the humor always so much a part of her.

"I…uhm…" Howie eased closer, looking everywhere but at the brothers. Then he locked his gaze to Brian, hands before him as if to ward off disaster. "I'm so sorry, Brian. This is all my fault. I really dropped the ball. It truly slipped my mind with everything I had going on at the time. I'll fix it."

Talk about a what-the-fuck moment. Brian didn't have a clue what he was talking about. Before he could utter a puzzled, "What?" Ceci tucked her arms over her chest, cocked out her hip, and stared him down.

"You're married? *Married?*"

Brian snapped to his feet, eyes shooting what he wished were laser beams at Howie. "Goddamn it! You were supposed to handle it. You promised to handle it all. Piece of cake. Said and done. We *depended* on you."

Howie waved his hands. "I forgot. I'm sorry. I had so much—"

"Enough!" He tried to soften his expression as he cupped his hands over Ceci's shoulders. "I'm sorry, Ceci. I thought… It was a long time ago. A weekend fling she and I both regretted by Monday morning. Howie said he'd take care of everything."

"And I will. I swear it," Howie quickly replied.

Ceci sighed. "The press is all over this. Someone started doing Internet research to see if we'd applied for a marriage license yet. They found the previous license in Nevada. Now the hunt is on for the 'mystery wife'—Alexandria Claremont."

Poor Lexy. She sure didn't deserve this.

Paul vaulted to his feet. "How could you forget you had a wife? How could you not tell us?"

Brian whipped around to face his brothers, all their faces so similar they could have been quads. Dispositions were another matter. "I didn't forget her." He'd never forgotten Lexy. In his mind she was always his favorite mistake. The true love of his life. "We were playing that gig in Vegas." The one that helped put them on the fast track. "We were all riding pretty high that night." On top of the world and ready to conquer all. "Lexy was a cocktail waitress. We met. Sparks flew and we got carried away and quickly realized that. I didn't tell any of you because it was a stupid thing to have done."

"Which appears to be a common affliction for you," Paul replied.

Brian doubled his fist. Caz and Nick jumped up to intervene.

"Everyone needs to calm down." Nick pushed Brian toward his chair.

Brian moved, but he refused to sit. Instead, he gave the chair to Ceci. She sank into the depths, crossed her long legs, and stared at the wall.

"I'll fix it," Howie said again. "I've already located the woman. She's still in Vegas, so the paperwork should go through without a hitch."

That was damn quick work on Howie's part. Brian would give him kudos on that, but it wasn't enough.

"I wouldn't count on that." Caz resumed his former position, feet propped on the coffee table, hands folded over his stomach. "A lot's happened in the last ten years. We were all wild and crazy back then. We had next to nothing; now we have it all. Nevada and California are both community property states. As his wife, Alexandria Claremont is entitled to half of everything Brian's earned during the marriage. And I hate to even think what the IRS will do when they discover the tax returns filed for both of them the last ten years are wrong."

Nick snorted. "IRS got their cut and then some. To pursue Brian and this woman—"

"Her name is Lexy," Brian snapped. *Beautiful, sweet, hot as hell Lexy.*

Paul snickered. "Yeah…the little woman."

Brian reared back a fist. Paul mirrored the stance.

"Stop it!" Ceci yelled. In all the time they'd known her, she'd never once raised her voice. She sure had their attention now. "Just stop it," she added more softly and covered her hand over her eyes to hide what Brian suspected were tears. He couldn't stand seeing her hurt this way.

Squatting before her, he touched her knee. "It'll be all right, Ceci."

She shook her head. "No, this was a mistake. All of it." She was on her feet a second later and aiming for the door.

Howie barred her way. "If you break off the engagement now, it'll look bad."

Ceci laughed. "Yes, things are looking so wonderfully great right now, aren't they?" She sidestepped him and darted from the room.

Paul took off after her like a shot.

Howie worried his hair some more. "I'll get this fixed, Brian. I swear it. I have her address and phone number and—"

"No. I'll take care of it. This has screwed up her life, too. I'll talk to her myself. She deserves that much. If she wants more, she can have it." Brian would give her anything and everything to make up for this breach of trust. But he wouldn't lie that the thought of seeing her again made him feel all mushy inside, worse than a kid on a first date.

"But—"

"I said no." He thrust out his hand. "Give me the information."

"But—"

"Now."

Howie pulled his notepad from his back pocket, flipped it open, tore out the page, and handed it to him. Brian snatched it from his fingers and walked away. What in the world did he say to Lexy after all this time? By now she most likely had heard the news. He hoped she hadn't remarried. Talk about a major screw up. Howie was thisclose to being fired. If it had been Brian's decision alone, he would have done just that.

As he came into the bright living room, Brian spied Paul and Ceci on the back patio by the pool. He'd wrapped her in comfort. Eyes closed, she rested her head on his shoulder. By rights, Brian should be the one consoling her. Thank God Paul was there to help him out. He could always count on Paul to do the right thing. If he'd let Paul know about Lexy from the start, they probably wouldn't be having this problem now. He'd make it up to Ceci later. Right now, he had to contact Lexy.

Brian took the stairs to the second floor two at a time. It wouldn't take long to throw together a bag. He'd become an expert at packing the last several years, always living out of a suitcase or on the tour bus. He'd go to Vegas, explain things face to face...

Indecision weighed him down. He couldn't just show up on Lexy's doorstep. Not only was it rude as hell, the paparazzi would be staking out the place, waiting to capture a reunion and all the drama that went with it. But a phone call felt cold and impersonal.

He stared at Howie's notes. Lexy's street address, where she worked—Convention Services for the Galaxy Hotel and Casino—and both phone numbers. There was no easy way to do this. Maybe it was better for all concerned to let the lawyers handle it.

Yeah...that's not cold and impersonal.

He fingered the paper and wondered if he'd recognize her. His memory held an image of brown hair and eyes that sparkled with life. A killer body that molded perfectly to his. And three days of crazy hot sex that had yet to be duplicated in all these years.

Great. Now he had a killer of an erection to deal with. He palmed his cock and adjusted the length against his fly. Other images flashed through his head—Lexy on her knees before him, nimble fingers unzipping his jeans, her hot mouth surrounding him.

Call first. Definitely call.

Brian picked up the cordless and punched in her work number…and just as quickly disconnected. What if someone else answered? Word would spread like wildlife that Brian Tristan had called her. They'd be inundated before either of them had a chance to breathe.

Who was he kidding? Paparazzi lay in wait already as he debated the best course of action. And how the hell was he supposed to think straight with a telephone pole swelling his trousers?

He tossed the phone to the bed and hot-footed it to his bathroom, unzipping and stripping as he walked. His dick felt desert-hot as he wrapped his fist around it. He remembered the tangle of white sheets, her silky hair shifting through his fingers, how damn tight and wet her pussy felt when he plunged into her. Brian had thought of her so many times over the years. How could anyone forget such a perfect weekend? If only they hadn't been so impulsive. If only they'd been in different stages of their lives. Yeah…he'd thought about it a lot. Day and night, especially at night, when he was wrapped in the arms of a pale substitute for Lexy, lost in the fantasy it was her.

He shoved his trousers to his ankles and fondled his tight balls, while his other hand flashed over his cock. He couldn't remember the last time he'd been this hard, this desperate to come. Through lids half-closed he watched pre-cum ooze from the tip. The image of full lips, a sensuous smile, and a talented tongue washed over him. Lexy could suck cock like nobody's business, make him wait until he thought he'd die, then suck him dry until his balls collapsed.

Brian shot his load into the green towel dangling on the bar, then braced himself with one palm against the cool tile wall while he tried to catch his breath. Reporters and photographers were going to hound them no matter what. Maybe a phone call would settle everything without them ever seeing each other, but it felt like the coward's way out. He'd man-up and go to her, make it all right, and explain to her husband or boyfriend—a woman like Lexy Claremont would have been snagged long ago. And at that moment Brian regretted again that man wasn't him.

Lexy *was* his favorite mistake, but the mistake hadn't been in marrying her. The mistake had been letting her slip away, and it wasn't a favorite anything. *Dumb, stupid, impulsive.*

Pulling in a breath, he hauled up his clothes and tossed the towel into the laundry hamper. One step after the other took him back to his bed and the phone staring up at him. He stuffed Howie's note into his pocket, grabbed his overnight bag, and walked out the door.

CHAPTER 3

Who is Alexandria Claremont and why has Brian Tristan kept her a secret all these years? The world wants to know and yet no comment has come from Mesquite, their manager—the very high profile Howard Ramsey—or Brian's brand new fiancée, Ceci Powers. The silence is deafening. The tight-knit brothers are definitely closing ranks on this one. We'll have more as this story develops.

Lexy Claremont kept her head down, gaze focused on the floor as she hurried across the reception room and on to her office, which she realized was way too far away. The blare of the television set followed her every step of the way.

How long before one of her coworkers decided to drop a dime on her? And it seemed like today every single person who worked in the Galaxy Hotel and Casino watched her. Those who knew her best were also putting together pieces of a much larger puzzle. She prayed they'd keep their mouths shut, although that bigger revelation, too, was only a matter of time.

Thank God Ethan didn't hear the report. The TV was set to the Cartoon Network this morning while they prepared for school and work. On the drive to his school, she'd kept the radio off so they could talk about stuff. It was part of their routine and made for a great start for the day. Her feel-good mood crashed the second she pulled away from Ethan's school and turned the radio on.

Lexy didn't know whether to hyperventilate or throw up…or both. She did know their home would be inundated by the end of the day, if it wasn't already. Reporters would talk to her neighbors; they'd find out where she worked…if they didn't already know. Her number one priority—her priority from the get-go—was to protect Ethan as much as possible, even if it was only for a few more days.

She swung into her office and shut the door behind her as she fumbled for her cell phone. It was right there, a hand grasp away, and yet she was shaking so badly she couldn't snag it. The night cleaning crew had left the vertical blinds open. Harsh desert sunlight beamed in from the east, making it impossible for her to see anything in her small office, much less the numbers on her cell. Using her thumb, she dialed J.D. Hempstead's number as she strode to the window to shut out the day. Right now, he was her only hope.

He answered on the first ring. "Well, well, well…how's your morning going, Mrs. Tristan?"

"Don't start with me, J.D." Her sigh should indicate her stress level for him. J.D. knew her well enough to recognize the signs.

"I thought you were divorced or annulled or whatever." Obviously he wasn't going to respect her being on edge.

"I thought so, too. His manager was going to handle everything."

"Apparently he didn't."

"J.D…please. I need your help."

"What in the world could I possibly… Ethan."

Lexy closed her eyes. "Yes. Could you please run to my house and get his things for a couple of days? Then get him from school?"

J.D.'s own sigh drifted through the line. "Lex, I just pulled a double-shift, all-nighter setting up for the arriving conventioneers. I'm really not in the mood to play 'hide the kid.'"

"J.D.—"

"No, Lex. It's wrong. I told you that before."

On more than one occasion, too. It had been a frequent source of strife for them for the brief time they were a couple, and more so now that they were best friends since J.D. was more vocal about his displeasure. J.D. insisted father and son know each other. But Lexy…

"We've been over this a thousand times," she said. "I don't want Ethan exposed to that life."

He snorted. "And as I've said during every one of those thousand times, that excuse might have worked in the beginning, but not once during their career has Mesquite or any of the Tristan brothers ever been linked to questionable behavior."

Lexy pinched the bridge of her nose. She knew that, too. The knowledge ate a hole in her resolve and her stomach. But she couldn't very well show up on Brian's door ten years after the fact and present their nine-year-old son to him.

"He's a gifted child, Lexy. We both know that. Music runs thick in his veins. He's the image of his father. One of the teachers is bound to have heard the news this morning. Your last name is all over the place this morning; couple that with his looks and that's that. Baby, it's already too late."

Tears blinded her. Her makeup was history, just like her carefully structured life.

"Look at it this way," J.D. went on. "This revelation could work out very well for you. Oh, he'll be pissed, no doubt about that. But Ethan and Brian need to know each other. Brian's become very wealthy the last ten years. As his wife, you're entitled to—"

"No!"

"At least child support," he finished.

"No. There's nothing I want or need from Brian Tristan."

Silence. And then, "We both know that's a lie. He was the ghost in our bed for the entire time we were together."

Lexy let the tears fall. She couldn't deny it. It was crazy to still be hung up on the guy. It was one wild weekend that should have been wiped away with the years. They'd agreed it was a mistake. He had his career to pursue. She had college to finish and her own career. Both paths were going in opposite directions, not even on a parallel course. Then two months later she was left staring at a blue stick while she puked in the bathroom.

She wanted to say her decision was a gut-wrencher. It wasn't. Lexy didn't want her baby exposed to the rock world life. Sex, drugs, road trips, no stability. She didn't want Brian to think she'd trapped him either. It was better this way, her way. And with each year, each day that passed the lie became both harder to maintain and more imperative.

The memories were the hardest. How one weekend could absorb her thoughts forever was a mystery. Yes, it was the weekend she conceived her child, their child. How could anything so precious be considered a mistake? She suspected she'd built the event up in her mind. No sex was that good, that earth-shattering, that all-encompassing. Yet she'd hear Brian's voice in Mesquite's music and it felt like Brian was making love to her, like the words were meant for her and her alone. She'd see his picture on TV and in magazines, the grown-up version of their wonderful son, and see the man Ethan would be one day. And want him. Crave him. Remember how his body filled her. His laugh. His touch. His kiss. His co—

"Are you still there, or are you just ignoring me?" J.D. asked.

Lexy sniffled and flicked tears from her cheeks. "I'm sorry, J.D. You deserved so much better than me." He did, too. J.D. was one hell of a great guy. He'd loved her. He loved Ethan. But they worked better as friends than as lovers. She wanted J.D. to be happy. Wanted someone who would love him back as fully as he loved. Another of those rough decisions made by mutual agreement.

"Damn it, Lex..." He puffed out a breath. "Don't expect me to lie and tell people Ethan's my son. That's not fair to anyone."

"I know, J.D. I'll fix it."

"Quickly."

"I...I don't know how to reach Brian."

He snickered. "Oh, I have a feeling someone will find you. Too much is at stake. It might be a good idea if you and Ethan stayed the weekend at my house. Maybe it'll all blow over by Monday. If not..."

"Then I'll suck it up." It wasn't fair to J.D. to stay any longer.

"You might also want to think about calling your parents and giving them a heads-up."

One disaster at a time. "Yeah, I'll think about it."

"Hmph. That's a fuck-you if ever I heard one. I'll grab some things for you while I'm at your house. See you after work. If anything comes up, give me a shout. I'm going to try to catch a few hours sleep while I can before I pick Ethan up. What the hell, I'll flirt with his teacher some more. Maybe that'll make her notice me."

"Thank you, J.D. I..." He really did deserve someone great, and Ethan's teacher was way more interested than she let on. "Just thanks."

She was still shaking as she ended the call. Not just her hands—her whole body. Any minute now she'd be face-to-face with her past. Brian would be standing before her, close enough to touch, close enough to kiss, close enough to wrap herself around.

Lexy laughed at herself. Who was she kidding? Brian had people to handle stuff like this. He was engaged to the very beautiful Ceci Powers, his girlfriend of one year. He was probably pissed as hell to learn he was still married to Lexy. She was worried for nothing. All she had to do was sign whatever papers were necessary relinquishing any and all claim to his fortune and she'd be good to go.

Then why did her ego feel bruised at the thought of Brian not bothering to come himself? God, she was a mess of contradiction. If she didn't focus on something else, she'd drive herself nuts. *Work.* Work was good. That was why she was here.

Before Lexy could boot up her computer, there was a tap on her door and then it opened. Her boss braced himself in the doorway, filling it with his linebacker bulk. He didn't look happy.

"Go home. Take personal time. There are two reporters in our lobby, and that's two too many. These people multiple like rabbits. I want them gone." He arched his eyebrow. "Unless you can spin this to our benefit by booking Mesquite for—"

She cut him off with a cold stare.

He smirked and shrugged a shoulder. "Can't blame a guy for trying." He took a step inside. "Do you need anything, Lexy? Anything I can do? Anything at all."

She appreciated the big guy's offer. "No…I don't know. This is as much a shock to me as it is to everyone else. A weekend fling ten years ago that got out of hand. Brian and I both thought it was annulled."

He scratched his head. "No hope for that now. Not considering how long it's been."

"He's engaged. I doubt he'll care."

He shut the door quietly behind him, then sat on the edge of her desk. "He will when he finds out about Ethan, Lexy."

"Maybe he won't care." That was a lie. She knew Brian would care. In the brief interludes between bliss, they'd talked about kids and dogs. Everyday stuff.

"As cruel as this is going to sound, he'll care a lot. The very nature of his public persona forces him to care. His people won't allow his image to be tarnished. If anyone comes out of this on the shitty end of the stick, it'll be you."

"I had my reasons, Don."

"I'm sure you did." He was sympathy personified. "Hopefully, he's the type of man to listen and understand what those reasons were, Lex." He patted her trembling hand. "Go home. Take care of this. Want me to drive you?"

"No, I can manage."

"It might be a good idea to get Ethan out of the line of fire. Maybe he could stay with your parents. Or you two could go up to our cabin for a couple of days, let the lawyers settle this."

The last thing she wanted was a battle between lawyers. "J.D. is taking care of Ethan for the moment."

Don nodded. "He's a good guy. A shame you two never… I guess that would have really made things a mess now, wouldn't it?"

"A moot point," she muttered.

"I suppose it is. Whatever happened to the two of you? It seemed like J.D. loved you, worshipped the ground you walk on."

Lexy didn't need this guilt. Don knew better than to deal that card her way. She glanced up at him, eyes amazingly clear for the first time in hours. "I didn't love him back the way he deserved, Don. That was hardly fair to J.D."

She grabbed her purse and slung the strap over her shoulder. "Thanks for the time off. I'll handle this as quickly as possible and do my best to make sure it doesn't interfere with the office. Call me if anything comes up, and I'll run right in."

She hurried away without another word, head up this time, but still ignoring the whispers around her. Her heart ached, fear gripped her soul, and her traitorous body relived that long-ago weekend. And for the first time Lexy honestly admitted to herself that the reason she couldn't love J.D. was because she loved another man. A man she'd spent a hot weekend with. The father of her son.

It was crazy, insane. They'd jointly decided it wasn't going to work. None of that mattered. She'd loved Brian Tristan from the second their gazes met. Loved him more when she saw him reflected in the eyes of their child. Nothing would stop that. Not even his hate.

CHAPTER 4

What was wealth for if a man couldn't use a little of it to his advantage? Brian had gotten a ridiculously expensive, last-minute ticket on a puddle-jumper and arrived in Las Vegas in record time. If he'd driven, he'd still be stuck in Los Angeles traffic and looking at a four- to seven-hour trip.

Brian watched Lexy's house from the safety of his rental car. For now, the anonymity of the rental, along with the haphazard disguise of sunglasses and a *Lakers* ballcap, kept the growing swarm of reporters from noticing him. He'd also taken the precaution of parking as far out of the line of sight as he could without losing his view of Lexy's cookie-cutter house. But as the crowd continued to grow, so did his chance of being seen.

Lexy lived in an older subdivision. Every house looked about the same—desert tan with white trim, single floor, sand for a yard with a few drought-resistant plants and trees. Few neighbors peeked out to see what all the commotion was about. Brian supposed that meant they were either at work or asleep from having worked the night shift. Or maybe they didn't give a shit. All of it worked for him. A nosy neighbor would blow his cover in a heartbeat. But he supposed it was only a matter of time before some reporter got the grand idea of knocking on doors for information about Lexy.

He wondered how she was doing at work. Hotel security would probably nip any reporter interference in the bud. He wondered if she was captive in her home, afraid to leave for fear of being cornered.

Brian tapped his finger on the steering wheel while he considered that possibility. The garage door was shut. The drapes drawn against the desert sun. Barricaded against the world or just not home? He picked up Howie's note from where he'd placed in it the console. This close he could call, find a way to sneak in to see her so they could get this resolved.

Screw that. I'll walk right through the crowd if I have to.

He reached for his cell, then jumped when it rang. Brian snatched it up—Paul—and let it go unanswered. He didn't want support right now, or to listen to a lecture—the most likely reason for his brother to call. He wanted Lexy.

The admission went deep into his veins, heating his blood, even while goose bumps shivered over him. He'd always wanted Lexy, *still* wanted her. How many times over the years had he been with a woman and fantasized it was her? How many times had he wondered how she was and fought the urge to contact her? Always something interfered with him doing so—mostly fear she wouldn't remember him, fear she'd found someone else, fear he had never been more to her than a weekend tryst. So much better to keep the fantasy and perfection in his head than have it destroyed by reality.

They were so young and crazy back then, pulled apart by divergent career paths and the logic of others weighing their consciences. Lexy had his heart from the first glance and his body not long after that. Brian never wanted either of those back. He'd wanted to think of himself forever in her arms, buried in the heat of her body…even while he fucked someone else. Or rather *especially* when he fucked someone else.

How could he do this to Ceci? The answer was obvious—he couldn't. As much as he hated the idea of never having Ceci in their lives again, marrying her to keep her close was wrong. Ceci had a right to all the love and happiness marriage could bring. She wouldn't have that with him.

He punched in her number with his thumb, then disconnected when he found her line was busy. Almost instantly, his cell rang with her calling *him.*

"Hey," he answered.

"Hey." She sounded so sad.

Brian didn't blame her and prayed she understood what he was about to tell her. "You're not covering so Paul can yell at me, are you?"

Ceci gave a small laugh. "No, he's off on a tear, determined to find out all he can 'about that woman.'" She imitated Paul to perfection. "I called because…" A sigh filtered through the line. "I can't marry you, Brian. I like you. I enjoy the time we've spent together. But last night I just felt cornered. I didn't want to accept your proposal, but I also didn't know what else to do. Please understand it has nothing to do with anything else. I've been in tears since last night, not overjoyed. The news this morning seemed like the perfect excuse to call this off. I realized after you left that I shouldn't need an excuse. If I don't want to marry you, that's all the reason I need."

Relief poured through him. "That's why I was calling you, Ceci. Last night was awkward. I didn't want you embarrassed by it all. The thought of not having you in our lives hurts."

"Oh, Brian, I'm not going anywhere. You're my friend."

There was a beat of silence, then they both started laughing softly.

"I'm so glad I called you," she said.

"Me, too. In fact, I'd tried to call you a second before you got through."

"It's one weight off my shoulders."

Brian frowned. "There are more?"

Ceci sighed. "Yeah, but I think you've just given me the hope and courage to fix that one, too."

"I'm here for you."

"And I appreciate that more than I can say."

"Enough to keep Paul off my ass while I get things settled?"

"I think I can manage to keep him occupied."

The smile in her voice warmed him as they ended the call. That's when he saw Lexy. His heart tripped over itself, cock swelled his pants, and mind went blank. She was headed his way in a cherry red Mazda four-door something. Dark glasses guarded her eyes, but nothing could disguise that beautiful face, that long brown hair. He could feel his fingers sifting through those silky strands, wrapping them around and around. Her lips—full, yet not overblown—with the color only nature could produce. Brian could still taste them after all these years. Could still feel her clutched to him.

She drove by her house without a glance in its direction. She flexed her fingers around the steering wheel. Long, red nails gleamed in the sunlight. He'd loved the feel of them down his back, loved how she'd tease his testicles on their points while her tongue did sinfully delicious things to his cock.

Nearer now, she slowed, and he knew Lexy had seen him. He

wondered if her breath caught like his, or if she was cursing the fact he'd dare to show up on her doorstep.

Brian whirred his window down, determined to get her to stop and not caring who saw. All he knew was that he couldn't let her go by without saying something, without some contact. He held out his hand. Lexy pulled even with him as her window rolled down.

"God, you're more beautiful than I remember." Too late he realized he'd spoken out loud. "Please don't have your husband come beat me up."

Lexy's lips quirked into the semblance of a smile. "That'd be a trick I'd like to see. No boyfriend. No husband. Other than you, apparently."

"I'm so sorry, Lex. Howie promised he'd take care of everything."

"He took care of things all right. Your fiancée must be furious."

Brian shook his head. "No fiancée. Ceci and I realized we were caught up in a moment and being too impetuous."

"Yes, been there, done that."

He felt himself flush with embarrassment. He didn't want her thinking this was a pattern with him. "No, no," he added quickly. "We truly are just friends."

"With benefits. Like I said, 'Been there, done that.'" She looked away. "Sorry, not my place to judge. It's been a long day already and promises to be an even longer night." She jerked her head toward the reporters parked in her front yard. "I don't want anything, Brian. I'll sign whatever you want me to sign. No lawyers. No press. No hassle from me whatsoever."

He could drive away and have his people—not Howie—take it from here. End of story. Except Brian didn't want it to be the end. He wanted her back in his arms, in his life where she should have been all along.

"Is there somewhere private we can go to talk?" he asked. Like for an hour or two, or a day, or week, or... "Pick anyplace in Vegas. Anyplace in the world. I'll cover it."

She looked from him to her house and back again. "I think I can arrange something at the Galaxy. Follow me. With luck I can arrange for us to go up through the freight elevator, but I doubt we'll be able to keep our presence a secret for long. There were reporters gathering there when I left amid whispers and speculation from my co-workers."

"I'm so sorry, Lex."

To his amazement, she smiled. It cut a path from heart to balls and back again.

"Maybe they'll look at me with newfound awe for a while. I'm sure it will last as long as it takes for the next coming thing to distract them." She tucked the earpiece to her cell phone in place. "My boss said he'd do whatever he could to help me get this resolved. I'm going to take him at his word. Once we get in the suite, we'll be good to go."

"Lead the way."

CHAPTER 5

Lexy couldn't catch her breath. It was a wonder she managed to dial Don's direct number. Seeing Brian in person tossed her back in time to that very first look and devastated her all over again. No wonder she'd fallen for him back then. One glance and she was head over heels once more, and so wet she could have quenched the hot Vegas landscape for the next million years.

"You okay?" Don answered.

She imagined him poised at the edge of his desk ready to leap to her aid. "Is that offer of help still on the table?"

"Yes. Of course. You know it is."

"My front yard is covered in reporters. I ran into Brian down the street. Can you arrange a private—"

"Done. I'll meet you at the service entrance." He ended the call before she could say thank you.

Lexy flexed her fingers around the steering wheel, praying her sweat-slicked hands wouldn't make her lose her grip. She glanced in the rearview mirror at Brian. He'd come to her when anyone else in the retinue associated with Mesquite could have handled this. That meant what? Everything or nothing at all?

Not engaged. Just friends. The things those words did to her libido, including setting her heart up for a big fall. Even if, by some quirk of fate, Brian had even a teaspoon of affection left for her, it would all be gone the instant he found out about Ethan. Maybe it wasn't desire that had her body all awry; maybe it was fear. Lexy counted heavily on press reports that Brian was easy-going and even-tempered. After all, what did she really know about him? It was one weekend ten years ago.

She swallowed the lump of emotion stuck in her throat. A weekend filled to the brim with talk and the best sex she'd ever had. They'd shared everything about themselves that weekend, body and soul. School, family, first kiss, first love, ambitions, goals, plans for the future. The only blank was the last ten years. A big ten years as far as Brian would be concerned.

How could she begin to explain? It all made sense at the time. In less than two months after they'd parted, Mesquite's first album went gold. They were on a rocketship to stardom and heading there at light speed. Lexy had picked up the phone to try to contact Brian. She got his manager instead.

Howard Ramsey wasted little time showing up on her doorstep, offering her obscene amounts of money to "make this little problem go away." When that ploy didn't work, he'd used guilt. *"Think how this will affect Brian and Mesquite. His brothers have worked hard for this moment. Do you really want to have it destroyed by an illegitimate child?"*

Even then Ramsey withheld the information that he'd never bothered to get them the annulment as promised. Most likely he'd forgotten or brushed it aside as insignificant, as inconsequential as the baby she carried. Lexy hated him then and hated him now. He'd manipulated her like a master, built on her fears for her child. Rock stars. Drugs. Booze. Roadies. Sex everywhere. Living on a bus. And what if Brian out and out rejected the baby? Lexy could have dealt with him rejecting her, but their child? Lexy couldn't bear for her baby to know that hurt.

Little did she realize she was hurting Ethan just as much by not naming his father. But by the time she realized that, it was too late to undo the damage. Even worse when she saw how musically gifted Ethan was, how much he idolized Mesquite—his own blood. Posters everywhere. CDs. She was damn lucky no one had made the connection by now. But her luck had just run out. Her world was imploding faster than an out-of-date casino on The Strip.

God, you're more beautiful than I remember.

Another skip to her heart. Lexy would treasure the compliment for the moment because Brian sure wasn't going to feel that way soon. She'd tell him everything the minute they crossed that threshold and were safe behind closed doors.

Lexy cranked up the air conditioner to high and recirculate. Sweat still trickled down her back and between her breasts, soaking her emerald green silk blouse. At least the short sleeves gave her some relief, otherwise she'd be sporting pit stains to rival a construction worker. *So much for cool and collected.* At this point she couldn't manage calm either. Shaky, submissive, and pleading? No problem.

Brian did a great job keeping up with her in Vegas traffic. He was never more than two car lengths behind her.

"We have a son, Brian."

Lexy shook her head. Too abrupt.

"Brian, I have to tell you something."

No, still not right. Maybe the aggressive approach. After all, this was his manager's fault.

If only. She was a presumably responsible adult and should have made sure this was taken care of years ago, no matter how fearful Howard Ramsey had made her. Being pregnant, working, and trying to finish college wasn't an excuse. Puking every day for three months. Losing weight, then gaining it like crazy. Labor pains. Raw nipples. Yes, she could turn this around if necessary. Unfortunately, her conscience wouldn't let her.

Pictures. Her wallet was stuffed with pictures of Ethan. They'd sit, discuss everything like rational adults. She'd take out the pictures and explain everything, accept the rage she clearly deserved. He'd never believe his trusted manager had played her. She couldn't believe it herself. She'd listen to Brian rant and rave, call her every name in the book if he wanted. And when he was done, when she was sure harsh words wouldn't touch Ethan, then—and only then—would she allow Brian to see him. Because Brian would want to see him.

And Ethan?

"Oh, God…what an ever-lovin' mess."

Lexy fumbled for her cell phone and dialed J.D.'s number.

"I'm all locked on," he told her when he picked up. "I got out of there by the skin of my teeth, but so far, so good."

"I'm with him, J.D.," she said softly.

"Whoa. No shit? As we speak?"

Smart ass. "We heading back to the Galaxy. Don's arranging a private place where we can talk."

"Good, because this thing is spiraling out of control fast. You might want to call the school and let them know."

"And risk one of them telling Ethan?" Lexy winced at her shout.

J.D. didn't deserve her frustration.

"Sweetheart, by now I'm sure someone already has."

He hung up without another word. Lexy stared at the freeway ahead of her, cars wavering in the flood of unshed tears. A quick call to Ethan's school relieved her worries there. No reporters. No incidents of any kind. J.D. would be there when school let out, and Ethan would think it was nothing more that a playdate with his big buddy. Maybe this confrontation would be all over by then and she could pick Ethan up herself. Although the thought of drawing attention his way from those lurking reporters made her think twice about that.

One problem at a time.

Lexy exited the freeway and circuited around the Fremont Street Experience. Brian was right behind her. She expected google-eyed fans to notice him and go nuts, but no one seemed to pay much attention to those driving by. They eased into the rear of the Galaxy Hotel and Casino in anonymity. Don lifted her a wave from the loading dock as she and Brian parked nearby. No security hovered about. No shipping clerks lurked. That alone could build suspicion, but it was standard procedure for those times high profile celebrities visited the Galaxy. Few would think much about it.

Brian swung a duffel bag over his shoulder as he exited the vehicle, then strode her way to open her car door. Her heart raced a little more. He'd been that way before—opening doors, holding out her chair. She looped her fingers around her voluminous purse and thanked him with a smile.

It was a tight squeeze with them wedged beside the next vehicle. Brian could have moved back to give her more space. Lexy could have excused herself and waited for him to do so. Instead, she stretched from her car and brushed her body against his. Contact ignited wildfire in its wake. She edged away at their joint intake of breath, but her hard nipples still strained to reach for his equally hard chest. Lexy didn't remember him being that rock solid, and here she thought she'd memorized every detail.

His cell phone shattered the moment. Brian jerked it from his pocket, glanced at the display, and ignored it.

"Ceci?" she asked, then cursed herself for the flare of jealousy.

Brian smiled and shook his head. "Paul calling to yell at me, most likely, and I don't want to hear it."

She clutched at the purse strap over her shoulder to keep her hands from wandering where they really wanted to go—on Brian.

"Ceci and I spoke earlier," he said. "We'd come to the same conclusion that we're great friends but nothing more."

"Because of me."

Brian reached for her face. His hand hovered there as if he was undecided on whether he should or should not touch her. "It's always been because of you, Lex. I regretted our decision soon after we made it. I could barely stand it within one day of you being out of my sight. I've thought about you constantly, wanted you…loved you," he finished on a whisper.

Her heart twisted. Her gut churned. Breathing? Not possible. "Then why didn't you call me?" she pushed out.

"I thought it was what you wanted."

"I wanted *you*, Brian." The words squeaked out past the ever-growing lump in her throat. "I wanted you back from the second you walked out the door." His hand still hung in the air between them. She wanted those fingers against her cheek, his breath against her ear, his lips covering hers.

"Then why didn't *you* call *me*?"

Here it was. The big revelation. Not the most ideal location for it, but Lexy wasn't going to put it off anymore. "I did, Brian. Two months after I last saw you. I got your manager instead."

His hand fell as he jerked back. He smacked into the car beside them, but didn't seem to notice, or maybe he was using it to hold himself upright because Lexy had never seen anyone this gut-punched. Dread crept down her spine.

"You spoke to Howie?"

"Yes. I called as soon as—"

"Tick-tock, kids," Don called out.

"We'd better go." She shut the car door and led the way to the loading dock steps.

"Howie never told me, Lexy." His stride matched hers. So did the devastation in his voice.

God, what had she done? The excuse that she'd made the best possible decision at the time based on the facts she'd had didn't wash. She'd been young, frightened, heart-broken—which was partly her fault… Hell, it was all her fault. She should have dug in her heels, insisted she speak to Brian, stormed the defenses around him and spoken to him face to face. But then, there was the whole sex, drugs, and rock and roll fear. A mother's fear for her child, played on by a man she now realized had his own agenda.

Somehow Lexy had the presence of mind to introduce Brian to her boss. Don's natural charm soothed the awkwardness that had welled up between them. He escorted them to the freight elevator, punched in the code for the upper level suites, even walked them to the room. Lexy gripped the lifeline of her purse straps and watched Don slide the keycard into the lock.

He swept the door open to the two-story suite. Smoky windows gave them a beautiful view of Vegas without the glare of sunlight. At night it would be amazing with the neon lights all aglow. A spa bubbled gently in the corner. A basket of fruit and bottled water sat on the bar. A spiraling staircase led to the three bedrooms on the second level. She'd always admired these suites, but they were way out of her price range.

"Everything is compliments of the Galaxy," Don said.

Brian offered the semblance of a smile. "My sincere thanks, but I really don't want you to go to that expense. I'll gladly pay for everything. In fact, I insist. It's the least I can do after you went to so much trouble to ensure Lexy and I had privacy."

Don tilted a nod his way. "Thank you. I'll make those arrangements with you later in order to ensure your continued privacy." He let himself out without another word.

Lexy sank into the deep cushions on the sofa and finally let her purse drop. Words…she needed words. Courage would help, too. She jumped when she heard Brian's duffel hit the floor. Her heartbeat thumped with every step he took to the door and back, skipping a little when she heard him click the security bolt in place.

She fumbled for her wallet. Pictures, that's how she'd start. *This is why I called, Brian. I was pregnant with our son. His name is Ethan.* The image of his father and uncles.

Tears were blinding her again. Brian had cared. Had wanted her. All this time. So much time wasted. And in thirty seconds all that affection would be gone, and with it any hope for a future. She'd take Brian's anger and shoulder all the blame, let him get it all out. Nothing more was going to interfere with his relationship with Ethan.

What if he sues for custody? Lexy damned the devil sitting on her shoulder whispering in her ear. She buried her face in her hands and ordered the monster away.

"Hey, hey." The sofa sagged with Brian's weight. Strong arms wrapped around her shoulders and pulled her into his embrace. "No crying, sweetheart." Soft kisses delivered by hot lips brushed her forehead. "It's all past. We can start fresh. Hey, we're already a step ahead. No need to worry if I'll ever pop the question."

Lexy knew he meant it as a joke. God help her, she tried to laugh. It came out a sob instead.

"Aw, baby, no."

He slanted his lips over hers and gently kissed them. Her stomach somersaulted. He could have shoved his tongue down her throat and tickled her tonsils and it wouldn't have had as great an affect as this did. Lexy melted against him, remembering so well how devastating his sweet kisses could be. Was it so bad to want more, to have one moment in the sun before reality crashed down?

Brian rolled her into his arms until she was cradled on his lap. Lexy kicked her shoes off and draped her arms around his neck. She toyed with the soft hair at the nape, lips parted in anticipation while he nibbled first one and then the other. His hot hand skidded up her thigh and over her hip. Lexy tucked herself as close as she could, screaming at herself to be patient when she felt the beat of his erection against her other hip.

He cupped her ass, mapping it over and over with the sweep of his hand, while his lips still plundered hers. She savored every second, even though all she wanted was to rip her clothes off and spread wide beneath him. She opened her mouth more, silently pleading with him to come inside. He did…the barest tip of his tongue touching hers. Cream gushed between her thighs, pumped there by her pounding heart and pulsing clit. She whimpered. God, she couldn't help it. She loved him. She loved him so much.

Brian captured her bottom lip between his teeth, then the top one. His tongue traced the outline of her mouth, circled over the corners, paused and then…

Lexy moaned when he slid deep. She welded her body against him, kissing him as hard as she wanted him to kiss her. Her heart ached. Her body wept. All of her cried for the loss of years.

There was a tug at her waistband—Brian pulling her blouse free. Just as she thought that, his hand spanned her lower back. A thumb circled her skin, warning her in which direction he was moving. Why did he have to take so much time getting there?

Lips kneaded her harder when she tried to wiggle into the caress. Tongue lashing around hers quelled her protest. Then fingers, callused from a near lifetime working a guitar, brushed her midriff. Muscles quivered, shooting shock waves of want out in all directions. And still he kissed her.

His hand drifted lower, and Lexy nearly splayed open her thighs to let him have at her. But he went no further than her belly where the first blouse button awaited his orders. He flicked it through its hole like it was nothing, then moved up to the next...and then the next, until the edges fluttered to her sides. Ragged breaths shuddered her breasts. And his kiss went on.

Brian pushed her blouse off her shoulder, then feathered his fingers down her arm and over her stomach once more. He wandered upward, outlining the lower edge of her bra, playing her with the same precision he would one of his treasured instruments. He traced around to the hook. Again, a flick released it. He snagged the strap and slithered it down her arm. Lexy wiggled the other side down and off. He groaned, the first sign his control wasn't as strong as he pretended, then tossed blouse and bra aside.

His hand shook as he cupped her breast. She swallowed another groan from him and scooted off his lap to the sofa, pulling him until he stretched out beside her. His rough thumb teased her nipple. He broke the kiss with her moan and wrapped his mouth around his new prize.

Lexy clutched his head to her chest and damned the tight skirt that kept her from wrapping her legs around his hips. She hooked her leg around his calf, rocking her pelvis into the steel-hard erection nudging her crotch. With each suck, more waves radiated downward until she was sure she could come from that alone.

He raked his mouth from one breast to the other, his palm covering the first. Fingers kneaded while he sucked the second and thrust his pelvis into her. She clutched at his back, finally able to snag his shirt with her nails. She yanked it up. Brian released her long enough to pull his head free of the garment. His hair tousled, eyes half-closed with lust, he plunged into another soul-searing kiss.

He rasped her nipples over his chest, groaning more and more with every move. His grasp wasn't so measured now. Frantic fingers plucked at her skirt's stubborn zipper. Lexy lifted up, trying to help, and pressed the cleft of her pussy harder into his cock.

Brian broke the kiss on a rough growl. He clenched her hips to still them, but instead rocked into her more fully. Lexy fisted her skirt and hauled it to her waist. Legs free, she wrapped them around his waist. Brian growled again and rolled to his heels. Cupping her ass, he lifted her higher, slammed his mouth over the crotch of her pantyhose, and sucked.

Lexy cried out and arched into him. Her clit was so hard she swore it'd poked a hole through panties and hose. She fumbled to pull them down. Brian grabbed the waistbands and jerked with her, tugging until he had no choice but to move his mouth. She jerked her legs free and reached for him.

Brian stared down at her, pants for breath steaming the air between them. His cock swelled his trousers, straining the zipper to bursting. How could she resist? Reaching out, she palmed his erection.

His eyes rolled back in his head with his groan. Brian clamped a loose grip around her wrist, stilling her movements. Then he wrenched down his zipper, pushed trousers and shorts to his thighs, and shoved her hand toward his testicles. Lexy cupped his hard sac, rolling his balls in her palm, promising him more with the finger wedged against his anus. Pre-cum moistened the tip of his cock. She waited until his gaze caught hers, then glanced at his dick and licked her tongue over her lips.

She sat up, pushing up backward, taking the lead, lips poised to suck his long, thick cock. Brian stabbed his fingers in her hair and lifted his hips to her waiting mouth. Then just as quickly pulled her head away.

"I want to do this in a bed," he gasped out. "Treat you right. Like the lady you are, not in a heated fuck on a sofa. Although"—he grinned—"that has its merits, too."

Lexy smirked and ran her finger up the underside of his erection. "I don't know who you think you're fooling. You're just trying to buy time because you're so close to coming."

He chuckled. "Very true. And so are you." Without warning he rolled her back into her original position.

She squealed with laughter, then sighed with pleasure when he wedged his knee against her wet pussy. Lexy rocked her clit over him, the hair there adding to her friction. Brian traced his cock up to the valley of her breasts and wedged them around it. Only the glistening tip peeked from the top. She shoved a pillow beneath her head for support and sucked his cockhead between her lips.

Brian's groan tightened her clit. She clamped her thighs around his knee and rode him hard. He pumped wildly between her breasts, mindless grunts and groans falling from his lips. She tried to watch the pleasure on his face, to focus on sucking and twirling her tongue around him. But the feel of his balls cushioned at the base of her breasts, the hard knee wedged into her crotch, the wildness, the orgasm building and building…

She jerked her head forward as she came, swallowing as much of his cock as she could. His balls clenched an instant before salty cum drenched her mouth. She drank it down, milking him with her tongue, until he slumped.

Lexy expected cuddling or distance. Instead, he pulled in a deep breath, stood, and dragged Lexy to her feet. "Upstairs, woman. That bed is screaming our names."

He snagged his duffel bag and fondled her ass, guiding her up the spiral staircase with kneading fingers that kept wandering to her crack. He kissed her shoulders, her neck, biting, licking, sucking. By the time they topped the stairs, Lexy was primed. So was Brian. A new erection prodded her back, leaving a trail of pre-cum over her lumbar.

Lexy grabbed the bedspread, hauled it down, and crawled onto the mattress. She lay back to watch him, fingers toying with her hard nipples while her gaze adored him. She felt the slice of his duffel zipper deep inside. The crinkle of condom packages stoked her higher. Brian took his gaze off her long enough to rip open one packet, then his gaze caressed her body as he rolled the rubber in place.

The blast from his cell phone startled them both, but other than a little jump, neither of them bothered with answering or questioning if it should be picked up.

She reached for Brian when he crawled onto the bed. Strong arms embraced her first, then his body cradled hers into the soft mattress. They lay like that, forehead to forehead, arms around each other, his erection hard against her soft belly. Magic, and neither of them wanted to pop the sweet bubble surrounding them.

When he shifted lower, Lexy parted her thighs and lifted her pelvis to him. Brian paused, his cock one jab away from being inside her. Instead he slid farther down. His gaze worshipped her during his journey. His touch was gentle, awestruck, as if he simply couldn't believe she was here. Lexy sure understood that feeling. She kept expecting the sweet dream to dissolve any minute.

She closed her eyes against a sudden rush of tears. It would end soon enough. She just wanted this one moment before everything went to hell.

She glanced down when she felt Brian part her folds. Without pause he twirled his tongue around her stiff clit. Lexy raised into the touch. He slid his fingers deep inside, stopped, and dared a finger in her ass. Groaning, she rolled into his gentle thrusts. One hand clutched the pillow beneath her head, the other furrowed into his hair, ready to nail him in place should he decide to wander off target.

He rolled the hard flesh between his lips, then flicked his tongue over it. Lexy couldn't think beyond that point. Orgasm lay on the threshold just out of reach. He played her body well, like they'd done this every day for all the years they'd been parted. In her mind, her fantasies, he had. Reality was so much more rewarding.

His thrusts changed tempo, harder, with more...precision. Then he sucked her clit and the climax rolled out of her and right into him. Lexy gasped with the sensation, suspended in pleasure as he drew the moment out to full completion. She drifted to the other side of heaven on a whimpered moan.

Brian released her with kisses and caresses up her body, until his lips were near hers. In one smooth motion, his cock and tongue plunged into her.

Lexy sucked in a breath and tossed arms and legs around him. She wanted to weep, wanted to laugh, wanted to scream with joy...wanted to come again.

He wedged his hand between them until his thumb kissed her clit. He rolled over it again and again. Kissing her like their lives depended on it. God knew her heart did. She dug her nails into his shoulders and rocked her hips into him, not so silently begging him with deep moans to fuck her. Brian groaned back, plunged deeper, then gave up.

He broke off the kiss and shoved his face against her neck. His forearm braced her from his full weight. His pounding cock made her take it all. His thumb made sure she didn't miss a minute of it.

Lexy nailed her heels into his butt cheeks, letting each demanding pivot of his body into hers take her on a ride that would have to last her a lifetime. He got harder and hotter, faster. Pussy muscles gripped him all the more. She could feel the climax in both of them, knew they'd make it together. And still it didn't prepare her for how wondrous that moment was.

They froze, straining into each other with the explosion. It swept them into a vortex, making them one, reminding Lexy why they'd been so great together before. They sagged into an embrace in the aftermath of their joint orgasm. She basked in his smile, his soft touch, his simple kiss.

"I love you, Lex. How could we have been so...misled?"

Frowning, she pulled back as far as the mattress allowed. "Misled?"

His damn cell phone cut off further conversation. Brian muttered a curse that Lexy echoed.

"Answer it. He'll never give up."

He rolled from her to grab it, and Lexy used that chance to dash to the bathroom. She shut the door as he snapped out, "What, Paul? What do you want?"

Hands braced on the sink, Lexy stared at her tousled hair and flushed cheeks. The image of a woman well loved. She'd wanted one last time and gotten it. The next time she looked in the mirror…

She pulled in a breath, squared her shoulders, and finger-combed the tangles from her hair. It was time. It was past time. She prayed for the right words.

CHAPTER 6

"Hello? Did you hear me?" Paul asked.

How in the hell could Brian not have heard him? The news still ricocheted through his head. He didn't even want to think about what it did to his heart.

"A kid, Brian. She has a kid. A son. *Your* son."

"I heard you the first time," he managed to say. Ten years…wasted.

"She lied, Brian. All this time. Hid him from you."

"Shut up, Paul. Just shut up. There's lying going on all right, but it might shock you who it came from."

"But—"

"Not another word." He ended the call, turned off the phone, and tossed it into his duffel.

The condom around his flaccid penis mocked him. He pulled it off, tied the end, and tossed it into the trash can. At least he'd become wiser about something over the years. Actually, he'd become wiser about a lot of things, his eyes wide open to more stuff as well.

When had she planned to tell him? *Poor Lexy. All this time, raising a child on her own.* Now he knew what she'd called Howie about two months after they'd parted. God only knew what the son of a bitch had told her. It made him sick inside. Physically ill to think that he'd been manipulated by Howie as well. A pawn. All for the all-mighty dollar.

How to fix this? Where was his son now? *School.* It'd only be a matter of time before the press found him. Maybe they already had if Paul knew. Maybe Howie had fessed up. Howie knew, Brian had no doubt about that.

He heard the toilet flush and then water running in the adjoining bathroom. How in the world could he broach this subject? Where should he start? He had a thousand questions. What was their son's name? Did she have pictures with her? Could he see him, be with him…be the family Brian had always wanted to have with her before someone else's money dreams had interfered?

He pulled his extra pair of trousers from the duffel and pulled them on. Lexy walked from the bathroom in mid-zip. She had a white towel wrapped around her, her hands clenched, red-rimmed gaze locked onto him.

"I have to talk to you, Brian. I meant to do so when Don left, but…" She dropped her chin and stared at the floor. A deep breath set her gaze back on him. "Perhaps it would be better if I showed you. I'll be right back."

She darted for the staircase. Brian waited a couple of heartbeats, then followed. It was obvious what she was going to tell him. If he hadn't been all over her the minute they'd stepped in the room, she would have already done so.

He reached the first floor to find her shaky hands fumbling with her wallet. *Pictures!* She'd been going for them when they arrived, too, and he'd interrupted her. He hurried her way, took her hands in his, and pulled her to the sofa with him.

"Look, Brian," her voice quivered. "Look." She thrust the opened wallet in front of him. "Ethan…his name is Ethan."

Now his hands shook as he cupped hers, folded his fingers around hers, and stared at the image of another Tristan. There was no denying his bloodline.

"He's nine. I…I…"

"It's why you called Howie."

"Yes." She flipped to another picture, then another and another, so fast Brian didn't have time to really look.

He peeled the wallet away from her. "Slow, honey, please. Let me see my son."

"You will, Brian. I swear it. I didn't…I thought…"

He dropped his hand to her knee. "Tell me what Howie told you."

She did so through tears and, with each word, Brian's anger toward Mesquite's longtime manger grew. Howie had stolen these years from them. No one else was to blame. They were young, afraid, impressionable. Howie fed on it all for his own greed. He'd made Lexy afraid of Brian's work, his life, never even let Brian have a chance. He'd tried to buy her silence, an…abortion.

"I didn't know what else to do," she finished. "I didn't know…"

"It's okay, honey." He draped his arm around her shoulders and pulled her against him, kissing her forehead, searching for the right words she also needed to hear.

"There was definitely rock going on the last ten years, but no drugs. Sex?" He shrugged. "Well, I guess we're only human. When a man's said goodbye to the woman of his dreams, I guess it's common to try to drown his sorrows in the arms of another. I imagine you've had—" *No, don't go there.* "I *know* you've had a lot on your shoulders. I'm mad as hell that I wasn't a part of your life, helping you."

He pulled her away to look in her face. "But I'm not mad at you. I'm mad at myself for being so gullible, for believing someone else's opinion rather than my own heart. I love you, Lexy. I regretted our decision to go our separate ways the second you were out of my sight. But Howie…"

He shook his head, not believing it himself. "Words like 'gold-digger, cheap cocktail waitress, looking for a big wallet and an easy ride' peppered his vocabulary. He was supposed to be the expert, the one to guide us all to fame. I asked him, 'What about love?'" Odd that he'd echo Paul's words from that morning. Odder still he didn't remember screaming that at Howie all those years ago until this moment.

"Howie said, 'There's no such thing and the sooner you realize that, the better off you'll be.'"

Brian's soul swam in her tears. "He was so wrong. It's all about love. It's all about you. It always has been. And now about Ethan. I want to know our son. I want us to have the life that was denied us. Do we have a chance, Lex? I'll give you anything you want. Do anything you want. Be anyone you want. For you. For Ethan."

She wrapped her fingers around his shoulder. "All I want is you."

Brian squeezed his eyes tight against tears and pulled her astride his lap. He held her tight, head tucked on his shoulder. God, he never wanted to let go.

"Come on," she whispered. "It's time you met our son."

"There's one thing I've got to take care of first." He kissed her, then pulled her from his lap. Lexy followed him up the staircase and sat on the edge of the bed as he retrieved his cell phone.

He punched it on, then punched the speed dial for Paul.

"I can't believe you hung up on me. You fucking hung up on me," Paul muttered.

"Tell Howie he's fired."

"Wh-what?"

"Tell Howie he's fired. If he wants to know why, tell him no one keeps me from the woman I love. No one keeps me from my son."

"Got it," Paul quickly replied. "I'll notify the record company and our agent. I'm sure one of them will have a replacement in mind. Want to set up interviews for tomorrow?"

"No, or you can do it without me. I want to spend some time getting reacquainted with my wife and acquainted with Ethan."

"Got it. Later."

"No questions asked?" Lexy dusted her nails over Brian's bare back.

Such an intimate gesture, and it felt so damn good.

"Not when it's family." He caught her hand, pulled it over his shoulder, and drew her down to the bed with him. "Do we have some time before Ethan's school lets out?"

"We do." She kissed his shoulder and stretched out beside him.

"Then tell me all about our beautiful child. And don't leave out a single detail."

CHAPTER 7

Any minute now J.D. would be at the suite door with Ethan. Lexy was nothing more than a bundle of nerves and guilt. Brian wasn't much better. He alternately paced and sat while he slowly scuffed his palms together, staring into space. Which doubled her guilt. On some level she wished he'd yelled and screamed at her, blamed her for keeping him from their son. That's what she'd been expecting, not that he would take equal blame, or that he'd fault Howard Ramsey for it all. Now that all of Howie's manipulating had come to light, Lexy had no problem pointing the finger at him. But she couldn't help wishing she'd been a little more stronger, had a little more faith in her own instincts. That wasn't going to happen again.

While they waited and sometimes paced in opposite directions, Lexy would look up at Brian—her husband—and feel a rush of love so intense she could barely breathe. She wanted to wrap her arms around him and never let go. Then he'd glance up and smile, walk her way and kiss her gently. She'd lean into his warmth, his comfort, contentment soothing her nerves at least temporarily.

Lexy watched him stare out the window, hands clasped behind his back, rolling on the balls of his feet every so often. There was no point in asking if he was in their lives to stay. That was a given. She wouldn't think about the years lost; it was the years ahead she'd treasure, years that could possibly bring them more children. But happily ever after existed in fairy tales, and this was reality. There would be rough patches. Commitment and compromise would see they weathered them together.

"There won't be much I can do about the reporters, sweetheart," he said.

She walked up behind him and wrapped her arm around his waist. "You and your brothers seem to manage well."

He draped his arm around her shoulders, pulled her to him, and kissed her temple. "We grin and bear it and just keep walking with a smile."

"Sounds like good advice to me. Polite indifference."

"Exactly, because they're always around watching everything you do. Ethan's school—"

"Protected. I'm able to pick him up every day. Galaxy has a child care program here for employees."

"I'd like to do that…pick him up and—"

A knock at the door cut him off. Brian whipped around, took one step forward, then stopped. "What if he doesn't like me?"

Lexy laughed lightly, stretched on tiptoe, and kissed his cheek. "Too late. He already adores you. Like I told you before, he's a big fan."

She laced her fingers through his and tugged him toward the door. His shaking hand reached for the handle when they stood before it. He pulled in a deep breath, opened it, and froze.

"Hi!" Ethan beamed a smile up at his father.

The joy in his face strangled Lexy's heart.

"Hi," Brian breathlessly replied. His smile matched Ethan's.

Ethan tossed his arms around Brian. Brian blinked away tears and held him tight.

"I knew if I wished hard enough I'd see you some day." The bright, shining face glanced up. "The kids at school said I was lying when I told them you were my dad. They sure know better now. Everyone was asking for my autograph today."

"You know?" the three adults asked in unison.

Ethan nodded. "Sure." He looked at Lexy. "I heard you and J.D. fighting about it all the time a long time ago."

"Let's…uhm…take this into the room," J.D. said, trying to usher them farther inside.

Ethan grabbed Brian's hand and pulled him in. "I play drums and am learning piano. I want to learn guitar next. I know all the words to all Mesquite's songs."

He started singing "Magic Waters," his voice so clear it sent shivers down Lexy's spine. Then Brian joined in. Ethan instantly moved into harmony with his father's melody. She brushed goose bumps from her arms, awestruck at the sound. She saw J.D.'s mouth hanging open and she managed to clamp hers shut. The last note hung in the air.

Brian's smile looked like it was going to split his face. "Perfectly executed! Well done!" He laughed and hugged Ethan tight.

Ethan rested his head on Brian's shoulder. "I practice all the time. I love to sing." He pulled up. "I even wrote some songs. I have them in my head, not written down. I don't know what I'm gonna to do when I get older. I understand my voice is gonna change. That sucks my whole game plan."

Brian laughed and ruffled his hair. She didn't realize how much the kid needed a haircut until now.

"It does for all of us," Brian told him. "But you just roll with it and come up with a new game plan."

"That's what I figured you'd say." He hopped back. "Hey, you wrote 'Magic Waters' for Mom, didn't you?"

Brian cocked his head to one side and cupped Ethan's shoulder. "I did indeed, son." Those brown eyes glanced up at her, making her insides quake. "Every song I write is about your mom."

Ethan bounced. "I figured that, too. I heard you say once that every song has a great love behind it, and I knew that was Mom. Her computer password is Brian. So I knew. I just knew."

Lexy spun away and pressed the heels of her hands in her eyes to stop the tears. Brian's arms surrounded her. She melted into the embrace and that kiss to her temple she treasured more with every second.

"It's okay, honey," he whispered. "Everything's going to be okay."

"I read all I could about you," Ethan went on. "I even wrote you letters best I could, but never heard back."

Brian turned around. "You sent me letters?"

"Yeah." He nodded. "To the record company. To some fan club. This older kid at school helped me search on the Internet and helped me write the letters. They always send me autographed pictures of Mesquite. I have a lot of those. Then I heard you had a manager. I didn't know what that was at first, but I figured he was important. This older kid helped me find his address."

Brian's hand tightened. Lexy rubbed his back in an attempt to keep him calm.

"Did he answer?" Brian asked.

"Nah." Ethan waved his hand. "Hey, let's go our house. I want to show you my stuff."

J.D. cleared his throat. "There are a lot of reporters at your place, Ethan."

The boy shrugged. "It's all part of being famous, right? We can handle it. Can't we, Dad?"

"We sure can," Brian's voice was rough with emotion. "We can handle anything together."

"Great. Let's go. J.D.'s got a date tonight with my teacher," he tossed out over his shoulder as he walked to the door. "She gets all giggly and red in the face whenever he's around. Girls are weird."

"He's very self-confident, isn't he?" Brian said with a laugh.

Lexy and J.D. grinned. "Oh yes."

"And talkative, too," J.D. added. He extended his hand to Brian. "A pleasure to meet you…finally. I'd love to hang around and get to know you better, but, as I'm sure you've heard, I have a dinner date."

Brian clasped the other man's hand. "Later then. Thanks…for everything."

* * *

Lexy tried not to laugh when Brian sank into the living room chair with a sigh. She knew the feeling well—the bliss of evening and the quiet that went with it. Silence descended when Ethan fell into bed each night in a sleep only the young truly knew.

Brian looked content, like he'd really meant what he'd said when he walked in the front door hours before—that her house felt like home. He apparently didn't care for the house he and his brothers had purchased, despite the cool recording studio in the back.

His presence felt right, perfect, the missing piece to the family puzzle. Lexy loved the way he'd handled the reporters outside, with dignity, grace, and calm. He'd requested they honor his privacy and that of his family. After a "thank you" and a wave, the three of them were safe behind closed doors. To Lexy's amazement, not one reporter infringed. They still hovered outside waiting for a photo op, but they stayed out of the yard.

Ethan's first priority was to show his dad everything he owned. Brian's priority was to make sure Ethan did his homework first. The reminder earned Brian a scowl, but Ethan nevertheless sat at the kitchen table to work. Brian stayed close to help, just in case, flipping through Ethan's school books and past assignments. He said nothing to interrupt Ethan's work, but his frequent nod and smile told the boy his father was pleased. Lexy swore his little chest puffed up with pride.

Once homework was finished, the two caved up in Ethan's room, talking music and guy stuff. They paused long enough for spaghetti and garlic bread, then were back at it. She listened from the hallway, not wanting to intrude on their bonding. Love brought happy tears as Brian set Ethan's words and music to paper, offering his own suggestions from time to time as the two hammered out their first song, "Finding You," a ballad about the search for the one you love. She had no doubt it would wind up on Mesquite's next album...with a little more tweaking.

Ethan had fallen asleep smiling at the sheet music by his bed. Even dead to the world, that smile remained. After his bath Ethan had told Lexy he was the happiest person in the world. She'd have to argue that point—privately, of course—she was beyond happy herself. And Brian looked like he could conquer the world and everything in it...once he relaxed a little from his whirlwind of an afternoon. Actually, the whole day had been like a carnival ride of emotions for both of them. Who knew it would end up so wonderfully?

Lexy popped the top on a beer and walked into the living room to join Brian.

"You look like you could use this." She tapped the cold bottle against his shoulder.

Smiling, Brian wrapped his fingers around it, then grabbed her hips and swung her onto his lap. "I could use *this*, too."

Hot lips covered hers, igniting the fire that parental responsibilities had kept banked. Lexy settled into his lap, smiling under the kiss when she felt his erection nudge her hip.

"Like that, do you?" he asked. The glimmer in his eyes raced her blood.

"Very much," she purred.

"And yet you give me beer. Are you testing my patience, my loyalties, or just trying to drive me crazy?"

Lexy wiggled against his cock. "I would never make you choose between your beer and your woman. I'll allow you to finish the bottle before I take advantage of you."

"Share?" He held the bottle before her.

"My pleasure." She licked her tongue over the lip, giggling when Brian groaned.

"Quit teasing."

"Only whetting your appetite for more."

"You won't have to work hard." He smirked. "Although I'd bet it's not as *wet* as yours is right now."

Lexy squealed when he pressed the icy bottle between her thighs.

"Shh," he said with a snicker, "don't wake him up."

She laughed. "Did he wear you out?"

Brian shook his head. "He does have a lot of energy. Wear me out? Not by a long shot. I enjoyed every single second. If he didn't have school tomorrow..." He took a drink, set the bottle on the table beside them, and cupped her hip. "He's very, very talented."

"Genetics." She'd never had any doubt about that. "I've encouraged him as much as I could."

"I'm sure he has his moments, but as far as I'm concerned, he's perfect. I can't wait for my brothers to meet him. My parents are going to be all over themselves with joy."

"I hope so." She traced the laugh line around his mouth.

"You and J.D. had a thing?" he asked. "Is that why you told him?"

"Yeah, a thing that didn't work out." She was embarrassed to admit the next. "I told him because I called out your name when he and I were..."

Brian winced. "Bad form, baby."

"I know. I can't believe Ethan heard us arguing over it."

"I can't believe how clever the little guy is. He even managed to track Howie down. Yet another nail in that bastard's coffin as far as I'm concerned."

Lexy wouldn't argue that. Standard policy for fan mail was to send out autographed pictures and that was that. But Howie knew about Ethan. On the off chance he'd forgotten, Ethan's letter wanting to contact his father would have tweaked his memory. His inaction made it patently clear Howie had an agenda of his own—covering his tracks, or rather, ignoring them completely.

"We've got a lot of years to make up for, Lex. There's no better time to start catching up than right now."

Clutching her tight, he stood so fast all Lexy could do was hold on and laugh, all the way to her bedroom. They fell to the mattress together, then Brian rolled away and to his feet.

"I'm going to shut the door, and by the time I get back you'd better be naked and ready." Two steps away, he shot her a frown over his shoulder. "Please tell me you have condoms."

Lexy grinned and started stripping. "Everything's in the drawer." She jerked her head toward the bedside table.

"Toys?"

"A girl's best friend." She tossed her skirt to his feet.

Brian grinned and hauled his shirt over his head as he hurried to the door. Her blouse landed on the floor behind him. He covered it with his trousers. Grinning, Lexy topped it with her bra and panties—she'd lost the pantyhose the minute they'd stepped into the house.

She crawled backward on the bed, shoving the bedspread down as she went. Long strides carried Brian back to her side, but it was the jutting erection that captured her attention. She tried to pose for him—a come-hither look with knee bent and rocking to and fro—instead, she found herself reaching for him, needing to touch him, love him, feel the muscles and heat beneath her fingers. Heart and body ached for him a thousand times over.

Brian pulled the drawer open and found the condoms under the magazines used to camouflage her stash. She envied the rubber he rolled into place, wishing it was her body that sheathed him. Goose bumps flared on his skin when she raked her nails over his ass. Leaning forward, she licked the path and followed that with little bites.

He groaned and pressed her back to the mattress. One plunge nailed her in place—the dildo he'd found spreading her wide. Dark eyes lit fire through her body. He worked the dildo out to the end, then deep inside, caressing his thumb over her clit as he did so. Lexy bit back a gasp. He traced the back of his fingers up to her breast, then flicked her nipple. The dark flesh stood at attention, waiting for more.

Brian pushed the dildo deeper. "Don't move, sweetheart."

He retrieved the tube of lubricant from the drawer. She jerked with the sound of it spurting onto his fingers. When he turned back her way, Lexy lifted her knees and parted her thighs. Brian wasted little time seizing his reward. She arched into the thrust of his fingers in her ass, rolling with the easy glide in and out. Fists flexed into the sheet, seeking something, anything to grab to keep from toying with her swollen clit.

Then he flicked it, liked he'd flicked her nipple.

Lexy whimpered and raised up for more. He plucked it between his fingers, pinching, while his other hand fucked her ass and the dildo filled her cunt.

"You know what I'm going to do to you, baby?"

She knew. God, how she knew. "Wh-what? Tell me."

"Tell you, or show you?"

No wonder legions of women screamed over his voice. The sound alone made Lexy want to come.

"Show me...please," she whispered.

He eased away to lube his cock. Lexy licked her lips and earned her clit another pinch. This time he didn't let go. He rolled the sensitive nub while he eased between her legs. Lexy brushed his thighs, soft whimpers begging for him. Hand guiding his cock, Brian pressed into the tight band of muscle. He took his time easing inside her nearly-virginal passage. She closed her eyes and gloried in the sensation. When he was buried to the hilt, he leaned over her, using his body to lock the dildo in place.

Lexy skidded her hands over his hips, up his sides, aiming for his back.

"No." Brian's voice cut through her haze. "Hands over your head. Clutch the pillow or I'll have to tie them. Just the thought of those beautiful nails going down my back makes me want to come so hard you'll taste it. And I want to fuck you long and hard first."

She did as ordered. Her over-sensitive nipples grazed the hairs on his chest. But it was Brian who groaned. Lexy couldn't help a victory grin.

He rocked back and tweaked her nipples hard. She thrust into him on a muffled cry. He pinched hard, rolling and pulling until she writhed beneath him. Every squeeze shot to her pussy. Muscles clamped around him and it felt like she was being fucked by steel. Her clit ached for attention. Forgetting her instructions, Lexy dropped her hand to her crotch, desperate to relieve the ache. A sharp smack against her hip reminded her of her place and doubled the agony.

"Oh, please, Brian...I need to come," she gasped out.

"I know, baby. Your cunt and ass feel like a molten vice." He fumbled for the drawer and she turned her head to see her bullet vibrator. "Put it where you need it, sweetheart," he said with a grin, and thumbed the control on.

Lexy smirked. *Two could play the power game.* Easing the shuddering little device between them, she kissed it over her clit, then shoved it beyond until it fell next to his sac.

Brian clenched his jaw against a groan. He ground into her ass and shoved his hand between them. His thumb danced over her clit. The control box fell beside them and kicked into high gear. Vibrations rattled through them.

"God, that's sweet," he gasped.

"Yes! Oh...yes!" Everything was tight, filled, swollen to bursting. The bullet promised relief, but kept it just out of reach. They pivoted into each other, grappling like...like...lovers reuniting. And just when Lexy was certain the end was in sight, Brian pulled back.

"Nonono!" She grappled for him, trying to pull him back.

He peeled off the condom, seated another, then removed the dildo, tossed the vibrator to one side and sank into her cunt.

"Yes!" she cried, nails latching onto his back.

He thumbed her clitoris, flicking it around and around as he pounded into her.

"Coming," she gasped. "Oh, God, Brian. I'm coming."

"I'm with you, honey. Give it to me."

Her body opened with the explosion, everything she was pulling him in while the sensation shot out. She held him tight, arms and legs locked around him. He buried his face in her neck, muffling the sound of his own orgasm as it quaked through him again and again. It felt like they floated on the crest for eternity before they sagged into the mattress panting for breath.

Then he kissed her...and kissed her again...and again. Emotion was too much to bear. She let the tears flow, knowing they were from happiness, knowing the future was theirs to grab.

"I love you so much, Brian."

"I love you, too, baby." He shifted her silky hair through his fingers. "I've missed you from the second we said goodbye. You are my heart, my soul, my reason for being in this world. I meant what I told Ethan. Every song I ever wrote, every song I ever will write, is for you. I'm going be with you forever and never let you go. I'm going to be by your side for all the brothers and sisters we give to Ethan."

Lexy inhaled his scent, male mixed with hot sex and christened with love. "We can do this. I have no doubts whatsoever."

"We sure can, honey. We have love."

And it was enough. It always had been, only now they were old enough and wise enough to realize it.

EPILOGUE

The revelations keep flying in the ongoing Mesquite saga. Yes, Brian Tristan is married and has been for ten years. Sorry to be a heartbreaker, ladies. Here's the kicker—he and wife Alexandria Claremont have a nine-year-old son. Word has it young Ethan is a chip off the Tristan block with musical talent that will one day rival his father and uncles. Can you say "Mesquite The Second Gen?" Today Brian made a statement through Mesquite agent Chuck Skinner thanking fans for their support and requesting his privacy in his family affairs. Rumors are flying about a magazine deal for a photo spread of the family with proceeds going to charity, but nothing's confirmed on the who or what of that yet.

On the heels of Brian's statement came another shocker. Long-time manager Howard Ramsey has been fired! It's been no secret the record company hasn't been happy with him from the beginning. No word out on what caused the split or who will be replacing him. The normally vocal Ramsey has been strangely mute on the subject.

Also silent and not seen is Ceci Powers. The was-she-or-wasn't-she fiancée of Brian Tristan hasn't been spotted in days. Some say she's licking her wounds. Others say she knew all along and was helping the high profile group protect Brian's wife and son from the spotlight. New insider sources say she's been hanging more with Paul Tristan aka Pablo than Brian. Hey, what's that about, girl? Come on, dish!

Guess we'll just have to wait to find out. You can bet we'll keep you up to date on all the scoop.

CRAZY ON YOU

CHAPTER 1

Paul Tristan knew the minute he first saw Ceci Powers that she was *the one*. Unfortunately, in the minute following that epiphany—before Paul could stride across the room and claim her—he'd discovered his brother Brian had already snagged her. He'd felt gutted with the knowledge, clutching an ice cold bottle of beer like it was his lifesaver. It'd offered as much salvation as a postage-size raft on the storm-tossed Pacific. The loyalty code of brotherhood had never been more difficult to uphold. Despite their disagreements, he and his brothers had always stuck together no matter what—a united force against the world and determined to reach their goals together. For the first time in his life, Paul regretted that stand, and yet he honored it.

Somehow he'd forced himself to smile when Brian walked toward him, hand possessively against Ceci's back. Somehow he'd forced himself to shake Ceci's hand during their introduction, despite the thrill that raced up his arm with their first contact. Somehow he'd let her hand go, even though all he'd wanted to do was haul her into the nearest room and fuck her brains out. One thing Paul promised himself at that heartbreaking moment was he'd make damn sure Brian treated Ceci like the golden goddess she was.

A year he'd watched them together. And in that year Ceci had become a part of their lives, integrating nicely with the family and the crazy life of a beyond successful rock band. A year of agony as he watched Brian ignore her more and more. And still Ceci remained, loyal to a man—his older brother—who truly didn't deserve her.

Now this.

Paul held Ceci as close as he dared, rubbing what he hoped were soothing circles on her back, muttering words of comfort, while she cried. She held him as tightly as he had that beer bottle the year before—as if she'd be lost if she risked letting go. He was partly to blame for her misery. If only he hadn't pushed Brian to move forward or let her go. But he'd been desperate for his own closure, desperate to see Ceci happy. How could he have anticipated *this*?

He wanted to knock the shit out of Brian right now. Hell, they'd come close to blows when Paul learned Brian had proposed to Ceci. Learning Brian already had a wife he'd conveniently forgotten about... If not for Ceci's intervention—she'd fallen nicely into the role of peacekeeper from the start—he would have decked his brother.

How could anyone forget about a wife? How could Brian not have mentioned her to any of them in the first place? Their parents were going to freak.

"Damn him!" The words exploded from his mouth.

Ceci lifted her head from his shoulder, fingers flexed against his chest. A little closer and her palms would cup his nipples; a little lower and her fingers would be able to toy with the hard flesh. The knowledge shot down to his groin, adding more substance to the cock already hard beyond capacity. An erection swelled down one leg of his jeans. That's what he got for not wearing underwear. He placed his hands over hers, intending to move them. Instead, he pressed them flat, stealing the sensation he longed for and trying not to show how much it devastated him that he couldn't have it honestly.

Tears glistened in her sea green eyes and spiked her long lashes. Mouth parted, lips moist and full. It mystified him again why Brian could not be all over her all the time. How Brian could drift away from her the way he had, when Paul ached for just a glimpse of her, held his breath for the sound of her voice, the kiss of her constant laughter, the light in her eyes.

"Don't," she said. "You heard him. He thought Howie had handled all the paperwork for the annulment. It was a wild, crazy weekend ten years ago."

"But he didn't *tell* us."

"Do you tell him every detail of your sex life?"

Ceci had him there. They weren't teenagers anymore. Sharing sex tales had ended in high school. But it pissed him off that Ceci was defending Brian. Where was her outrage, her fury? She was crying, for fuck's sake! Brian had broken her heart, and here she was, sticking up for him. As far as Paul was concerned, that was only more proof Brian didn't deserve her. But if Ceci loved him, Paul would do everything in his power to make sure she had him, even at the cost to his own heart.

"Don't you worry, baby. I'll make sure this gets fixed fast so you can have the wedding you want. I'm not going to let anything spoil this for you."

She pressed closer, angling her hips a whisper away from his. Too close for Paul's fragile libido. Her body heat poured over his pelvis. His penis pulsed with a life all its own, demanding he thrust forward and cover that last few millimeters between them.

"Paul…I…"

He braced his hands on her hips and gently set some distance between them before she could feel his hard-on, before he gave in to the urge to grind it against her. All he wanted to do was yank her back and kiss her, haul that cute black-and-white sundress to her waist and wedge her against the nearest wall while he showed her what loving a woman was all about.

She slid her hands over his shoulders, reclaiming the distance he needed. Paul's resolve started to crumble. It would be so easy to take advantage of her turmoil, so easy to swoop in and have her, to know what it felt like to be wrapped in her arms and buried in her heat. And lose her completely because of it. Because if he made love to her once, Paul knew it would never be enough. One of them would have to go, and since he'd be the one at fault…

He grabbed her fingers and took a small step away, holding her hands between them for a shield against his emotions and the aching cock that so wanted to throw caution to the wind and go for it.

"I know it won't be easy, Ceci. Hang in there. Women like Alexandria Claremont are a dime a dozen. I'm surprised she hasn't tried to ride the Mesquite gravy train long before now." He snorted. "She obviously didn't realize their marriage was still valid or she would have. Don't worry. She won't stand a snowball's chance in hell. I swear to you I'm going to find out everything I can about that woman. This is one fight she won't want."

She held on tight when he tried to walk away. "Paul, don't do this. Let Brian handle it. It's a relief actually."

"You're crying your eyes out and you call that relief?"

Ceci's eyes widened with his shout. Paul bit back an apology. If it helped keep them apart, that could only be a good thing at this point.

Right?

"I'll fix it for you, Ceci. I swear it, or die trying."

He strode into the house before he caved, before he spread her on the nearest chaise lounge and made his dreams come true. Before he told her how very much he loved her.

CHAPTER 2

The chaise's padded cushion whistled with Ceci's weight as she sank into it. Normally, that resulted in bawdy fart jokes from the Tristan brothers. No one was laughing today, and a good deal of the fault rested on Ceci's shoulders. How in the world had she let things go this far?

What little fire she and Brian had between them had fizzled after two months. She should have ended it then, but didn't because she liked the Tristan brothers so much she couldn't bear the idea of never being able to hang out with them. And then it happened. She'd fallen in love with Paul.

Ceci buried her face in her hands. She couldn't believe it herself at first. It had taken the distance of Mesquite's latest tour for her to finally admit the truth, but she knew before they left. Paul's was the voice she focused on when she listened to the band play. Paul's was the face she searched for, the smile she sought, the one whose presence she missed the most when the guys were gone.

Ceci made one excuse after the other for not speaking up: they were preparing their new album, they were preparing for tour, they were on tour, they'd just gotten home. All seemed like valid excuses at the time for not wanting to disrupt the group's harmony. But they were still excuses. Her primary reason for silence was fear. Once she told Brian it was over, she'd never see any of the brothers again.

The guys were tight. They had that all-for-one sibling code—blood thicker than water stuff. Which was great for a family, great for them as a group. That unity had helped them weather all the crazy ups and downs in this business. It just sucked for her. Tristans always stuck together. No one ever came between the brothers, especially a woman. Hell, they'd even bought this huge house together—a place she and Paul had found when Mesquite's financial consultant suggested they needed an investment for the millions pouring their way.

A door slamming jerked Ceci's head up. Someone had gone into the recording studio on the other side of the pool house. Considering the slam, it was most likely Paul. She'd never seen any of the guys this upset before, but then a secret wife would do that.

She smeared the tears from her cheeks. Her makeup was a mess. Ceci didn't need a mirror to tell her that. She should have handled this differently, too. Should have known Brian would never play anyone. The shock on his face when he heard the news was proof of that. She could have called, could have spoken with him privately, could have done any number of things differently—like not go along with the whole engagement in the first place. Now that made her feel stupid.

They'd both been cornered at the restaurant last night. Paparazzi hovered with their intrusive cameras at the ready, flicking shot after shot in the hope of catching something. Ceci had agreed to dinner with Brian so they could talk this out, end it. Why the hell she thought doing so in a public location was a good plan was a mystery. She knew better, but didn't realize her mistake until she arrived at Prestige. By then it was too late. Then the waiter delivered the engagement surprise to their table by mistake…

She rubbed at her temples. *If do-overs were possible…* Hell, she'd go back to the night she met Brian and walk the other way. But if she'd done that she never would have met Paul. God, she could still feel the heat from that first handshake. Her memory had somehow stored it for future reference, because that night her focus had been Brian and how nice it was to be having sex again after her long dry spell.

It was only later—months later, too late—she realized the impact that first contact had on her. The way Paul had clasped her hand, firm but not too tight. The hint of sadness in his brown eyes that he'd tried to temper with a forced smile. A handshake that now seemed to have been overly long, like they should have stepped into each other's space rather than avoid it. All these little things, all too late. All reminders that followed her to bed at night and drove her fantasies of Paul.

At least she'd had the decency to avoid Brian's bed once Paul filled her mind. Of course, Mesquite being on tour helped that issue. It didn't help her own, only fired up her dreams of seeing Paul again. Each time Ceci met up with the band during their four-month trip, her heart raced at the sight of Paul, her pussy throbbed and melted. And still she'd done nothing to shake up the status quo, except avoid sex with Brian. Funny, he'd avoided sex with her as well, pleading exhaustion. He didn't want her any more than she wanted him. The fire that pulled them toward each other in the first place had died as quickly as it had been ignited.

Then why in the world are you engaged?

Ceci covered her eyes as she leaned elbows on knees once more. Had he felt as trapped as she did last night? They might not have been lovers for a while, but they were still very good friends. Maybe he feared hurting her as much as she feared hurting…everything.

"No more," she said to herself. Better to hurt his feelings than to have them both live a lie.

Ceci pushed herself to her feet and hurried inside. She'd dumped her purse somewhere between the front door and the den—the brothers' favorite room in this sprawling house…after the recording studio in the back. She retraced her steps and found her black hobo purse right where she'd flung it just inside the den. Luck was with her—Caz and Nick weren't in the room. It looked like Howie had taken off, too, which was just as well since Brian was furious with the man, and his three brothers didn't look too far behind that same emotion.

Ceci snagged her purse and sank into Paul's big recliner. His scent wafted around her, wrapping her in the comfort she longed to feel in his arms. She tucked her legs under her and nestled deep into the soft blue cushion, while she plunged her hand into the depths of the bag to find her cell phone. No rehearsed speech. No hesitation. This had to happen now.

A flick of her thumb had the phone open before Ceci could pull it out. She punched "5" on speed dial. Nerves crawled over her skin. Hope deflated when the call went to voice mail. He would have flown to Vegas and had the device turned off. *Fine.* She'd wait him out…providing he'd return her call and not delete the voice mail unheard. If that happened, she'd keep trying until he finally answered. Or maybe go to Vegas and hunt him down.

Ceci quickly discounted that crazy idea. The tabloids had enough fodder to last them days right now. They didn't need any more. Even while the story played out within the confines of Castle Mesquite—and unknown parts of Las Vegas—the ever-present paparazzi hovered to pick apart the roadkill of their lives.

No, she was safe right where she was for the moment—curled up in Paul's big chair for two. She burrowed deeper and swiped the last remnants of tears from her face. Mascara and eyeliner blackened her fingers. God, Paul had seen her like this. Great image. *Too late to unring that bell.*

Ceci hopped to her feet and hurried to the nearest bathroom down the hall. The silence in the house haunted her. Like the place was holding its breath for what would happen next. That's how she felt, locked in perpetual wait mode, afraid to think beyond what she needed to do next. If she thought farther than that, Ceci would start dwelling on the ramifications of her actions—hurting Brian, losing them all, never seeing Paul again. Those fears had stymied her in the past. She couldn't allow them to do so again.

She shut herself in the bathroom and leaned against the door to steady her nerves. The brothers had designated this as *her* bathroom. Shades of black and pink Victorian designs embellished the room. No Tristan male dared cross the threshold. Makeup, curling iron and rollers, blower dryer, and various other necessities of feminine life filled the drawers in the vanity. Plush towels were stacked in the linen closet. Bath oils, bubbles, and soaps lined the shelf around a tub made for relaxing. Magazines and paperbacks were within easy reach. Her place, her nest. Her sanctuary in a household over-run with testosterone.

She'd also taken over the walk-in closet across the hall for clothes, shoes, whatevers. Paul had moved a chest of drawers in there for her use as well. The place was huge. She could have fit a twin bed in there if she wanted. From what she recalled of the Realtor's rambling accolades about the house, it had once been used as a dressing room for the bathroom opposite it. Ceci had wasted no time claiming it as hers.

She didn't realize how telling it was until now that nothing of hers was in Brian's room. In fact, they'd rarely slept in Brian's bed at the same time. Before they'd gone on tour, the brothers were rehearsing in the recording studio until all hours. Most of the time Brian slept on one of the sofas in there, or she'd fallen asleep listening to them work. Obviously, she and Brian did an excellent job of avoiding each other—politely, of course.

Another sigh launched her off the door and to the mirror. The damage to her makeup was worse than Ceci expected. She washed her face and left it at that. God only knew how many more tears she'd shed today. No makeup was better than smudged and runny.

Somewhat revived, she walked back to the den, kicked off her wedge sandals, and tucked into Paul's chair. It felt like heaven to sink into its depths. The only thing missing was—

"So are the three of you just about done dancing around each other?"

Ceci jumped at the sound of Caz's voice. Instinct made her check to make sure her dress wasn't gaping. He hovered in the doorway, making the space look insignificant. He was no larger than his brothers at six feet, but his personality always made him seem bigger. He stared at her with those Tristan brown eyes. The brothers could have been quads, they looked so much alike. The difference was in their personalities, and apparently the bear in this brother had been poked.

"What do you mean?" She tucked her dress down over her knees.

Caz stalked toward her. "You know damn well what I mean. Nick and I have watched the three of you play this game for almost a year. It's ridiculous. Brian avoids you. You avoid Brian. Paul makes cow eyes at you. You giggle over Paul and use every excuse to be near or touch him. You and Brian don't want to be together, and neither of you has the balls to speak up. You and Paul want each other so much I can smell it…and neither of *you* has the balls to speak up."

He was over her now, fists braced on the arms of the chair, nailing her in place with his presence, those eyes.

"Paul respects—"

"Bullshit," he spit out. "He's chicken. And stupid. The signs are clear enough if he'd open his fucking eyes and look. He can't see past the fact Brian had you first. It wouldn't matter to me, sweetheart. If I wanted you, I'd come after you. I thought of it a couple of times just to throw a scare into Paul and get him moving."

"You did?" Ceci didn't know how she felt about that news.

"I did," he said with a smile. "I would have, too…if I didn't find you too vanilla for me."

Ceci glared up at him. "I am not vanilla."

Caz's grin widened. "You are, too."

"Am not."

He cocked his head to one side. "Really? Prove it." He jerked his head toward the door. "Go get your man. Someone's got to make a move. Might as well be you. Do it, sweetheart. Go out there and go crazy on him."

Heat rushed her from head to toe. Ceci knew a blush went along with it. She stared at Caz, saw the continuing challenge in his eyes, and didn't know what the hell to do.

"I…I…" She shook her head. "Not until I talk to Brian."

"Need permission?"

His smirk pissed her off. "No. A clear conscience."

"Good enough." He pushed back and walked away, but only got as far as the door before he looked back. "Don't dawdle. Nick and I are sick and tired of the façade. We're prepared to take matters into our own hands if we have to."

"What are you gonna do?" she snapped. "Stick Paul's dick in me?"

"Intriguing proposition." Caz grinned. "Maybe you're not as vanilla as I thought."

He left without another word.

Ceci's body flamed with embarrassment. She fumbled for her cell phone and clutched it in her fist. She wasn't budging from this spot until she reached Brian. After that…

"One confrontation at a time," she told herself. Although the idea of going crazy on Paul made not thinking about it impossible.

I'll go out there and…and…

Good God! She *was* vanilla. The best she could come up with was flashing her tits.

Come on, you can do better than that.

Ceci punched redial on her phone, hoping against hope Brian would pick up and she could get that out of the way. All the fantasizing in the world wasn't going to come to fruition if she couldn't end it with Brian first. It was the right thing to do. Still, she let her mind wander while she hit the redial button over and over again.

It was Paul's thumb against *her* button…against her clit. Rubbing and toying it to the bursting point. Then his fingers inside her. His lips… Ceci frowned, trying to remember the last time she'd had oral sex. She shook the thought away and tried to dredge up the hottest scenario she could imagine, one where Paul would have no doubt she meant business.

What if Caz is wrong? What if Paul doesn't want you?

Ceci damned her conscience, but it was enough to deflate her confidence. She didn't know how long she sat there, dialing and dialing. It was the busy signal that snapped her back into the moment. Hope renewed, she dialed again. Brian answered.

"Hey." He sounded exhausted, beat down. Ceci could sure understand that.

"Hey," she replied. What if this news hurt him? She wasn't sure she could bear doing that. But was continuing to live a lie any better?

"You're not covering so Paul can yell at me, are you?" he asked.

Ceci gave a small laugh. "No, he's off on a tear, determined to find out all he can 'about that woman.'" She imitated Paul to perfection. "I called because…" She sighed. Though she hated giving him news like this when he had so much else to deal with right now, it had to be now. It wasn't fair to either of them otherwise.

"I can't marry you, Brian. I like you. I enjoy the time we've spent together. But last night, I just felt cornered. I didn't want to accept your proposal, but I also didn't know what else to do. Please understand it has nothing to do with anything else. I've been in tears since last night, not overjoyed. The news this morning seemed like the perfect excuse to call this off. I realized after you left that I shouldn't need an excuse. If I don't want to marry you, that's all the reason I need."

"That's why I was calling you, Ceci. Last night was awkward. I didn't want you embarrassed by it all. The thought of not having you in our lives hurts." He sounded relieved, happy even. It buoyed her spirits.

"Oh, Brian, I'm not going anywhere. You're my friend."

There was a beat of silence, then they both started laughing softly.

"I'm so glad I called you," she said.

"Me, too. In fact, I'd tried to call you a second before you got through."

"It's one weight off my shoulders."

"There are more?"

Ceci sighed, easily imagining the share-with-me look in his deep brown eyes. It was the look that had brought them together in the first place. She'd love to confide in him, but he had enough on his shoulders at the moment. And her feelings for Paul were something she had to resolve for herself. "Yeah, but I think you've just given me the hope and courage to fix that one, too."

"I'm here for you," he said.

"And I appreciate that more than I can say."

"Enough to keep Paul off my ass while I get things settled?"

"I think I can manage to keep him occupied," she said with a smile, and her imagination cranked into high gear.

CHAPTER 3

"How much longer are you going to be in here throwing a hissy fit?"

Paul didn't dignify Nick's smart-ass remark with a look. Someone had to see Ceci wasn't hurt. Someone had to make sure Brian was protected. If Nick and Caz were good brothers, they would have helped Paul research instead of doing…whatever it was they were doing.

"I'm not throwing a hissy fit," he snapped back. "I came out to the studio for some peace and quiet so I could search for information on the Internet about that woman."

Nick snickered and plopped down on the black leather sofa at a right angle to the one Paul occupied. "I don't know who you think you're fooling. You came out here to this soundproof building to yell and scream and rant and rave at the top of your lungs so Ceci couldn't find out how you really are."

The dig hit too close to Paul's heart.

Caz laughed and sank into the cushions beside Nick. "Oh, I think you hit pay dirt, Nicky."

Laptop balanced on his thighs, Paul swung his legs onto his sofa so neither of them would get any ideas about sitting next to him. "Shut up. I'm trying to protect our brother."

A half-truth. Paul was mad as hell at Brian and he didn't trust this blast-from-the-past wife either. Judging from Caz's snort, he didn't believe Paul either.

"She's got a kid." Paul turned the laptop around so they could both see for themselves. Neither looked.

"Yeah, it's all over TV." Nick shrugged. "Cute guy. Nine years old. Name's Ethan."

Paul stared at them. He'd been searching the Internet for hours and the news hounds already had the information? "He's probably not Brian's."

Nick's face lit up. "If Brian's not the father, then one of us is. The kid's the spitting image of—"

"I don't want to hear this." Paul cut his youngest brother off with a slice of his hand. "This is wrong. The woman's lied all these years. Hid the boy from Brian. She can only want one thing."

"Privacy?" Caz asked. "I swear to God, Paul, you hear, but you don't listen. Howie was supposed to handle the annulment and didn't."

"That doesn't explain why she hid the boy," he snapped.

"That's for her and Brian to work out." Nick scraped his fingers over his morning whiskers. "Maybe she didn't realize the boy was Brian's."

"You just said he was the image of a Tristan." Paul jerked the laptop around and shut it down.

"That doesn't mean she realized it."

"How can she not?" He was getting a headache on top of the one he already had trying to talk to these two. Why did they always have to reason things out?

"This is between Brian and her. All we can do is be here to support him." Caz slumped farther into the cushions. His gaze burned into Paul, like this was all Paul's doing.

"I don't want Brian blindsided by this. He needs to know he has a son before he meets with her."

"So, call him," Nick said.

God, did they think he was stupid? "I've been calling, but he won't pick up."

"Can't say I blame him. He's got enough on his plate without having to hear you lecture, moralize, and bitch."

"Do you blame me?" He slammed the laptop closed. "And you seem to forget there's another person's feelings involved here. What about Ceci? What about her feelings? She deserves way better than this." He stabbed his finger on the computer. "She deserves better than Brian."

"I agree." Caz stretched his arms high. His classic move when he was getting ready to make some smart-ass remark. "I thought about going for that myself."

Nick smacked his shoulder. "No shit? Me, too."

Paul glowered at them. What the fuck was this all about? This was the first hint he'd ever had that the two considered her more than a sister, a friend. And yet they sat there smirking as if she were a piece of ass to divvy up.

Caz grinned at Nick. "Imagine it… Her sprawled facedown over my lap, that smooth, sweet ass begging for a kiss of leather."

"Oh, yeah. I could go for that. Maybe we could do a little ménage thing. Wouldn't be the first time."

Paul tossed the computer to the cushion, swung his feet to the floor and was in their faces a second later, finger jabbing home his point. "If either of you little bastards touch Ceci, I swear to God I'll break every bone in your bodies."

Nick clutched his sides and howled. "Do you kiss Mom with that mouth? I've been on the phone with her for the last hour talking about all this. I should call her back right now. What would she think if she heard you calling her treasured youngest angels bastards?"

"What do *you* think she and Dad would think of what their freaking 'angels' do in their sex lives?" he yelled back.

"Don't knock it 'til you've tried it," Caz quickly countered. "Oops, sorry, I forgot I was talking to Mr. Missionary."

"You and Brian both," Nick added. "Obviously, neither of you ever snuck a peek at Mom and Dad in one of their wild moments."

Caz smacked his thigh as he cackled. "Oh, my God, look at his eyes, Nick. We've scarred Paul for life now."

His brain had just about shut down. The thought of Caz or Nick touching the woman Paul loved, quickly followed by the image of their parents engaging in any sexual activity was too much to absorb. He didn't know whether he wanted to slug his brothers or put as much distance between him and them as possible.

Paul flopped back to his sofa, shoved the laptop to the side table, and snatched his cell from beside it. "Get the fuck out of here. I've got to call Brian and warn him."

"*You* get the fuck out of here," Caz replied. "This is as much our place as it is yours."

"Besides," Nick added, "some of us might want to get some work done."

"Yeah," Caz said. "Two against one. We win. You go."

"Two against one." Nick snickered. "Ceci locked between us.

Mmm-mmm."

"Grow up." Paul vaulted to his feet, more than tempted to plow his fist in his little brother's perfect profile.

Caz palmed his crotch. "I'm feeling pretty grown up at the moment. Think I'll find Ceci and really help her dry those tears. By the time I'm done, she won't even remember Brian's name."

"Don't you touch her! Don't you dare touch her!" He clenched his fist around the cell. It was the only thing that kept him from swinging.

The mocking humor on their faces switched off.

"Why?" Nick asked. "Because you want her? It's obvious, Paul."

"At least it's obvious to the two of us," Caz told him. "It's obvious to Mom and Dad, too. You, Ceci, and Brian appear to be clueless. Open your eyes, brother. The woman wants you. The woman loves you. And Brian? He hasn't been a part of the equation for ten months."

They left him then, staring gape-mouthed at the wall, his body one raging hard-on. Ceci loved him? She wanted him?

I have to call Brian.

Paul glanced at the phone clutched in his grip. Logic was gone, but so was duty and obligation and loyalty. Caveman took over in all his primal glory, swelling his cock to unbelievable proportions. He didn't want to adjust it comfortably. He wanted to whip it out and run after his woman with his penis proudly waving before him.

Mr. Missionary my ass. If Ceci walked through the door right now, he'd show her fucking like she'd never forget. He'd have her down on all fours, pounding into her until they splintered a new fault line in the earth.

Then she appeared before him. Paul blinked, wondering if his sex-infused mind had conjured her. Her scent curled around him—gardenias and lust—and he realized she was no figment of his imagination.

Slow steps brought her nearer. Her gold-brown hair drifted down her shoulders, sea green eyes were bright, lips moist and full. Time slowed to a crawl. Everything moved in slow motion, or maybe that was his head playing tricks again, maybe freezing this moment for posterity, maybe making him finally realize all the time he'd wasted and that he should really treasure this second.

"I want you," she whispered.

Paul's legs quivered, threatened to give out on him. He wanted to collapse to his knees before her, wrap his arms around her thighs, wedge his face under her dress and peel her panties down with his teeth.

"I...I have to call Brian." He felt like an idiot. The woman of his dreams was within arm's reach, and all he could do was say he had to call his brother.

"I just talked to Brian. We're over and very relieved about it. We were meant to be friends, never lovers. You and I, however..." Reaching out, she slithered her hand under his T-shirt. Long nails raked over his stomach. The muscles bunched beneath her touch. "We...we were meant to be lovers."

Her thumb caressed his hard nipple as she stretched on tiptoe and covered his mouth in a kiss he felt all the way to his balls. The cell phone fell to the carpeted floor with a soft thud. Paul snapped his arm around her waist and anchored her to him. He fisted her dress and yanked it up, then stabbed his hand in her panties and squeezed her ass.

Ceci groaned and rolled her pelvis into his. Paul deepened the kiss, drowning in the sensation of their tongues thrashing. He wanted to eat her inside out...and he planned to do just that.

She tweaked his nipple hard, tearing a moan from his throat and his lips from hers. He tossed his head back and ground his cock into her, fingers kneading her butt cheeks with every push. Ceci feathered her tongue down his Adam's apple, nipped at his throat, then sucked at the base.

Paul tipped her off balance, caught her in his arms, and draped her onto the sofa. Another soft thunk landed her shoes next to the cell. She nudged her lips to his, begging another kiss with barely perceptible whimpers and flashes of her pink tongue. Paul sank into her mouth and wedged his pelvis between her thighs.

Ceci locked one calf around his hips. Her heat welded them together. She skidded her fingers over his ribs, down his spine, and plunged into his jeans as far as she could—which wasn't far enough for Paul. He wanted skin on skin, body in body.

He shoved her dress higher, desperate to feel her breasts, but the fire down below made the simplest of tasks impossible. He wanted to slow down and make this the best sex of her life. His cock had other ideas.

Paul rolled to the floor, kneeling before her open thighs. The smell of her pussy screamed to him. Her crotch was damp from her juices. Glancing up at her, he peeled her panties down. She tried to close her legs and move away. Her eyes widened, then puddled with tears.

"Oh, my God," she whispered. "I *am* vanilla."

If he didn't already love her like crazy, this would have cinched it for him. He kissed her leg, then rubbed his cheek over her soft skin. "My favorite flavor." He brushed the backs of his fingers over the inside of her thigh, then traced a caress over her muff. "I want to taste you, Ceci. I *need* to taste you."

"But…I was supposed to seduce you."

"You're here, sweetheart. It's all the seduction I need."

A sigh relaxed her. She pulled her bottom lip between her teeth. It nearly shattered what little control Paul had remaining. He tugged down the panties and just about came when Ceci lifted her leg free of the garment and draped her calf over his shoulder. He cupped her bare leg, rubbing up and down while he licked and kissed the bare flesh. When she kicked the panties from her other leg, he cupped her bottom and lifted her hips his way.

Eyes closed, he drank in the scent of her arousal. His mouth watered. Still, he took his time, savoring the feel of her skin beneath his lips, his cheeks, his tongue. It seemed he'd waited a lifetime for this moment, and Paul was going to treasure every second.

"I've wanted to make you come since the minute I laid eyes on you. Night after night I dreamed of making love to you. Just. Like. This." He punctuated each word with a kiss farther up her thighs, until the last breath was over her clit.

Ceci quivered. Her pussy glistened with arousal, thick and honeyed. Paul kissed her there, gently pulling the hard bud between his lips. She cried out, hips arched, thighs tightened around his head. He dug his fingers into her ass to keep from palming his cock. Wedged down the leg of his jeans, it damn well hurt…and helped keep him in check.

He curled his tongue around her clit, then lapped the juices from her folds. Soft cries urged him on. Taking his time took superhuman strength. He dared to explore lower, rimming the puckered flesh between her cheeks. Ceci jerked, then rolled into a moan that scored through his cock and clenched his balls. He couldn't wait a second longer. He nibbled his way up her labia, then sucked her clitoris into his mouth.

Ceci's breath caught. He felt the tremors deep inside and flashed his tongue over his prize. Thighs clamped his head in place. And she came. Came so hard she nearly pulled his orgasm with her. He stayed with her, easing her over the top and down the other side, when all he wanted to do was yank down his zipper and stab his cock into her viselike grip. Her pants for breath equaled his. She dusted her fingers over his head. When he glanced up, Paul saw a look so filled with love it quadrupled the ache in his crotch.

"I need you inside me," she whispered.

Paul swallowed hard. "I don't have a single condom in here, sweetheart."

Ceci gave him a sexy-as-sin smile. "I came prepared. Perhaps you need to do a little above-the-waist exploring?" She glanced down at her breasts, then back at him.

Paul grinned. "Oh, baby." He crawled up her body, taking her dress with him.

CHAPTER 4

Hot lips razed up Ceci's torso. She'd just had the biggest orgasm of her life, and all she wanted was another, preferably with Paul buried deep inside her pussy. She wiggled her dress over her head, then reached for Paul's shirt. He beat her to it, hauling it off and tossing it behind him. Her eyes drank in the sight of him. She'd seen him shirtless before and loved the chiseled planes. This time—finally—he was hers to touch.

She reached for him, but Paul seized her wrists in a loose grip and hauled them over her head. Her breasts stretched up for him, hard nipples begging to be released and sucked into his mouth. Paul held her wrists in one hand. He traced the edges of her black bra. Condom packages peeked out the top of each. He palmed both, then clamped his teeth on her bra and yanked it down.

Ceci's pussy clenched, clit woke up, and her mind shut down. She expected him to seize her nipple, make it his. Instead, he flicked the edge of the condom packages over it. She groaned and arched into him.

"Like that?" His voice dropped two decibels, low, determined, hot as hell. The fans went wild on stage when he did that. Every time Ceci would have to clamp her thighs tight to keep the ache at bay. Now…now she was splayed open, his to love.

"I-I do," she managed to whisper.

"And how about this?" He slapped his tongue over it, caught the tender flesh between his teeth, and rolled it.

Ceci jerked with the sweet shock and locked her ankles around his waist in a desperate attempt to feel his cock against her.

"Answer me, baby," he demanded, and bit a little harder.

"Oh, God, yes!" She tightened her grip around his waist and pivoted her pelvis higher.

A rough groan rumbled in his chest. "No fair." He pinched her other nipple.

Ceci thrashed her head from side to side. Her hips had a will of their own. She rasped her sopping pussy over the rough denim.

"Determined to have your own way, aren't you?"

"Determined to have you," she gasped out.

Another groan sent shivers over her. Strong arms locked around her. Paul pulled back, taking her with him. He sank in the cushion with Ceci straddled over his lap.

"Show me what you want, sweetheart." Mouth surrounded her breasts, suckling hard.

She cried out, fingers stabbing into his hair, holding on for dear life as he pulled and pulled until she felt the contractions in her clit. Just when she thought she couldn't bear another second, he released her…and took her other breast.

Ceci rocked over his erection, letting the rough denim assuage the ache in her crotch. His long, callused fingers probed the crack of her ass, exploring the place no man had dared go before. She trembled with a mix of anticipation and fear. Then he stabbed into her.

She moaned into the sensation and ground her hips onto his finger. She couldn't think beyond release, beyond the pressure building faster with each gentle thrust.

"Have you ever been fucked there, baby?" That voice again, demanding her orgasm in his tone. All she could do was shake her head.

Paul growled. "I'm gonna fuck you there, sweetheart. And I promise you it will be sweet. You'll come like you've never come before."

She rolled her clit over his fly, keeping time with his fingers fucking her ass.

"You want it, don't you, sweetheart? My cock buried inside you?"

Oh, God! The words. His voice!

"Tell me," he demanded. "Tell me how you want it." He sucked her nipple deep.

Ceci groaned.

"Tell me," he said around a mouthful of tit.

"I-I want you to fuck me." She gasped. *So close to coming!* "Hard," she panted. "Deep." She whimpered and rocked over him. "In...in..." She clamped her thighs around his as orgasm spilled from her.

Paul gave her little time to recover. He lifted her from his lap, forcing her to kneel before the other sofa. She curled her fingers into the leather cushion, lifted her ass higher, spreading for him. The sound of his zipper sliced through her. Pants for breath hitched with the whisper of jeans coming off. Body jerked with the rip of the condom package. And then he was behind her.

She pushed up, but Paul glided his hand up her spine, urging her shoulders back down. She settled with a tiny sound of protest and nestled her cheek into the cushion.

Hard cock probed her entrance. Eyes closed, she bit her bottom lip. Hands caressed her skin, like he wanted to memorize her. Or was it because he treasured this moment as much as she did?

"So beautiful." His voice touched what his hands couldn't—her core. "So soft. I always knew you'd feel this soft. But to touch you...mmm. I love you, Ceci. I've loved you from the minute I laid eyes on you." And then he slid into her.

Dual moans danced around the room. Nothing had ever felt as good as this. Only Paul's fingers moved, tracing her skin over and over, igniting tiny flames in their wake.

"I love you, too. I should have said—"

"Shh, baby." He draped himself over her, cradling her in loving arms, and brushed kisses over her cheek and shoulder. "We're together now and that's all that matters."

The declaration brought tears to her eyes. She fought against them falling, lifting her hips as best she could to Paul in silent invitation. He thrust deeper, then eased upright. Strong fingers gripped her hips, the tension in them revealing how tightly Paul struggled for control. Ceci tried to stay still, to give him the moment he wanted, but the feel of him so full and hard inside her made that impossible.

"Play with yourself, sweetheart," he ground out. "Make yourself come while I fuck you. I want to feel you clamped around my dick."

Without hesitation, she shoved her hand beneath her. Her clit was slick and still as hard as it'd been when she first walked into the door of the recording studio. But instead of massaging it as Paul wanted, she pressed her fingers around the base of his cock. Paul's groan made her feel all-powerful. Reaching farther, she cupped his hard sac. His testicles tightened even more. She weighed the heavy orbs, then kneaded her fingers around them.

He gasped and thrust into her cunt. Ceci flashed her fingers around his balls and aimed for the hole behind. His grip nailed her hips in place for another hard plunge. She gasped from the force of it, feeling the push in her womb.

"I wish I could suck your balls while you fuck me. Fuck your ass the way you fucked mine…until you come so hard I can see the jism behind my eyes."

Paul grunted and pounded into her. His testicles hugged his body, refusing to budge when she tried to urge them down. Heat poured over her hand. She felt the nerves twitch with Paul's impending release, yet somehow he managed to hold out.

Ceci looped her fingers around his sac and squeezed. Paul growled and shoved his hand to her clit. She pivoted into the caress and tossed her chin over her shoulder.

"Kiss me. Kiss me while we come."

He jerked free, rolled her to her back, and stabbed himself back inside. Lips covered hers, tongue matching the rhythm below. She dug her fingernails into his ass, urging him on. Paul grabbed her free hand and shoved it between them to her pussy. He rolled her fingers around her clit, deepening the kiss that helped sealed them. And when that wasn't enough, she locked her ankles around his waist.

Record plaques on the wall above rattled as the sofa smacked into the wall. Paul broke the kiss long enough to glance up, then covered her mouth once more and fucked her harder, faster.

Orgasm pooled in her belly, tightening everything. Her vaginal muscles clamped around the erection pounding into her. So hot. So hard. Paul's muscles quaked. He was close. She wanted them to come together. To have their bodies bless the union their hearts had already accepted. And then…

They broke the kiss on jaw-clenching groans. Ceci thought she'd never stop coming. He pulled back from a plunge, only to drive into her again as more cum exploded from him.

She damned the condom that separated them. She wanted his children…now! Wanted to feel them move inside her, see the joy on his face.

"God, I love you!"

Paul shot into her again, then sagged, finally spent. "I love you, too. So much. So very, very much." He settled them more comfortably on the sofa, combing her hair from her face, dropping sweet kisses to her cheek, her neck.

"I want to have your baby, Paul." She couldn't help the rush of words. She had to tell him.

The light in his eyes faded. Fear raced her heart. Paul wasn't even smiling. In fact, he didn't bother to look at her. His gaze was locked to the floor. She'd gone too far, got caught up in the moment.

Now what? Take the words back?

Never. This was how she felt. Ceci wasn't playing waiting games with him or anyone else. He needed to know where her mind and heart were from the beginning. If he couldn't deal with that, then it was best to know before things had gone any farther.

"Paul? I—"

His gaze snapped to hers, cutting off the words. "She has a child, Ceci."

Oh, no! Paul had a child with someone else? She couldn't breathe, couldn't think. "W-who?" she managed to ask.

"Alexandria Claremont." A frown pulled his eyebrows closer.

Relief flowed through her from head to toe and all parts beyond.

"A son, and she never said a word to Brian."

So like him to worry about others, even when he shouldn't. She brushed her fingers through his hair. "It's for them to resolve, love."

"I know." He sighed with the kiss she placed on his chin. "I just don't want him blindsided."

"You want to call him?" That's why he had been staring at the phone, debating what to do.

"Yes," he said with a slight nod.

"Then call."

"Thanks for understanding." His smile touched her heart. The man was devoted to those he cared about. It was one of the many things Ceci loved about him.

She missed the weight of his body the second he got up. Missed his heat, too. The air conditioning lifted chill bumps. She brushed them away and reached for her dress, while he rid himself of the condom.

"Oh…are we done?" he asked with a smirk.

Ceci grinned. "How about moving to a more private location? Like your bedroom." She feigned a gasp. "Or maybe my bathroom."

"Wow…you do love me. No man has ever crossed that threshold." He stepped into his jeans, grabbed the cell, and sat beside her to dial.

"If you're really good, I'll let you have bubbles in the tub." She tapped her finger to the tip of his nose. "No fart jokes."

"Yes, ma'am." He winked and punched the speed dial for Brian.

Ceci listened to it ring. On the third one, Paul shrugged and started to hang up. Brian's voice stopped him.

"What, Paul? What do you want?"

She rubbed Paul's thigh, hopefully keeping him calm. The brothers yelling at each other some more wasn't going to help anyone.

"She has a son. Your son. It's apparently all over the news."

Silence. Paul pulled the phone back to look, most probably checking to see if the call had dropped, then put it back to his ear.

"Hello? Did you hear me?" Paul asked. "A kid, Brian. She has a kid. A son. *Your* son."

"I heard you the first time," he snapped.

"She lied, Brian. All this time. Hid him from you."

"Shut up, Paul. Just shut up. There's lying going on all right, but it might shock you who it came from."

"But—"

"Not another word."

"He hung up on me." He stared at the phone like he couldn't believe it.

Frankly, neither could Ceci. Brian was the sensitive one, always concerned about hurting someone else's feelings. But he'd had a lot thrown at him today and that would break anyone. She sure understood Paul's drive to want to protect him, help as much as possible. She felt rather helpless herself right now, and more than a little awkward after throwing the baby plan out there.

"You've done all you can." She rested her chin on his shoulder and rubbed circles over his bare back.

"I know." Pulling in a sigh, he leaned back, draped his arm around her and pulled them both down to the sofa.

Ceci cuddled beside him, idly running her fingers through his chest hair, while he played with her hair. For the first time in a year she felt truly content. Still, she wished he'd say something, anything, about the kid thing.

"A perfect moment," she tried. "Just me and you."

"The first of many our whole life through."

They looked at each other at the same time.

"I should write that down," he said.

She wrapped her arm around his waist. "Later. I'm too comfortable. I promise I won't let you forget."

"Thanks, baby."

A kiss settled them deep into the cushion. Within seconds his hold on her loosened as he drifted off to sleep.

Later. They'd talk later.

Ceci had just dozed off when his phone rang. Mumbling a curse, Paul glanced at the display and then answered.

"I can't believe you hung up on me. You fucking hung up on me," he muttered.

"Tell Howie he's fired," she heard Paul say.

That jerked him upright and Ceci with him.

"Wh-what?" Paul asked.

"Tell Howie he's fired. If he wants to know why, tell him no one keeps me from the woman I love. No one keeps me from my son."

"Got it." Paul was on his feet, reaching for his shirt. "I'll notify the record company and our agent. I'm sure one of them will have a replacement in mind. Want to set up interviews for tomorrow?"

"No, or you can do it without me. I want to spend some time getting reacquainted with my wife and acquainted with Ethan."

"Got it. Later." He punched off the phone and stuffed it into his pocket. "You heard?"

"Hard not to," she said. "I never realized until now how far Brian's voice carried." Especially when pissed off.

"I've got to take care of this, sweetheart." He braced his hands on either side of her. "This won't take long." He kissed her quickly and hurried off.

Ceci stared after his departing figure, admiring the view. Paul had something to do to help make things right. It was what his nature demanded. But she couldn't help feeling disappointed that his focus had shifted from her.

Was it intentional? She'd like to think not, but she'd really put her foot in it. Any man would feel cornered with baby talk. He might love her like crazy, they might have known each other for a long time, but to throw that out there the first time they had sex? What the hell was she thinking?

Ceci hugged her arms around her midriff. Now that she had him, she never wanted to let go. But not wanting to let go was what had her in limbo this last year. She wasn't willing to live like that anymore. Now that Ceci had finally admitted to herself what she really wanted, she wouldn't settle for anything else. And she wanted Paul something crazy.

And they were going to talk about this.

Maybe if she tied him to the bed for a couple of days...

She smirked. *Now there's an idea.*

CHAPTER 5

Paul stopped long enough to wash Ceci's smell from his face. Personally, he wanted to bathe in her scent, but he really wasn't in the mood to have his brothers razz him over it. They'd already had their fun today…they didn't need any more. Besides, they had other things to concern them.

Howie Ramsey had been their manager from the start, which was obviously eleven years too long. Sadly, others in the business—even their own parents— had long suggested Howie might not have Mesquite's best interests at heart. An annual audit of financial records, suggested by their attorney, had showed nothing out of the ordinary. Every cent was accounted for. However, the feeling of something-not-quite-right lingered.

Discovering Howie didn't handle Brian's annulment ten years ago as promised now looked like the tip of the iceberg. Based on Brian's phone call, there was much more to the story, much more to Howie's manipulation. Though Paul, Caz, and Nick needed the details, the fact Brian wanted Howie gone was enough for them to get the ball rolling. Now if he could only find his brothers.

"Hey, guys!"

His voice echoed through the house. They really needed to put more furniture in the rooms. He'd loved the sprawling place the second he and Ceci had seen it. With the new album to build and the tour, the only rooms they'd devoted attention to were their bedrooms, the den, and the kitchen. And Ceci's bathroom, of course. They'd left the house for her to decorate, giving her carte blanche. It was slowly coming around to feeling like a home. She'd been taking her time arranging the décor, unwilling to spend a dime unless it was exactly what she wanted for them. Funny, she'd spent more time here than they had.

Paul stopped in the huge front room and really noticed the changes Ceci had made in the months they'd been on tour, touches they'd taken for granted. Emerald greens and gold brightened the beige carpeting. A sectional sofa curled in a great arc around a circular distressed walnut coffee table. He'd bet recliners were masked within the sofa.

It looked comfortable. It felt right. Like home. He could imagine the room filled with family and friends, laughing, visiting. A huge Christmas tree in the far corner, glowing with lights, seemingly supported by a mountain of gifts beneath it. Pine garland twined along the banister. Children playing, running around, more laughter filling the house.

He smiled at the image. *Kids. Brian's son and...*

"Oh, shit."

Yeah, that's right, buddy. You really fucked up.

"Well, it took you long enough to speak up," he snapped at his conscience. His baby. Ceci wanted to have his babies. And how had he responded? Paul wanted to smack himself upside the head. He hadn't said a word back, essentially ignored her and went on about Brian.

"You call us?" Caz asked.

Paul glanced up as he and Nick hit the bottom stair. "Yeah."

Nick jerked his thumb over his shoulder. "Caz and I were upstairs in his room watching one of the paparazzi across the way scale that old elm. They're growing thicker by the minute."

And it was only going to get worse. "Brian called. He said to fire Howie."

"Good." Caz punctuated the sentence with a nod. "Details?"

"I'm sure they'll be forthcoming," Paul said. "Something about Howie keeping Brian from his wife and son."

Nick snorted. "Which means Howie knew way more than he's owning up to."

"Exactly."

Caz plucked his cell phone from the pocket of his black trousers. "We'll have to plan this right. Call our attorney, agent, the record company—"

"And Mom and Dad," Nick added. "For the love of Pete, let's call them first. I don't want another hour-long discussion over why they weren't informed."

"Sounds good," Paul told them. He had a choice here—his family or Ceci. He loved them all, but Ceci was his heart, his future, the family he'd soon have…if he hadn't royally screwed things up. "I need the two of you to take care of all this. I have something else…" He held up his palms. "Just take care of this, please."

"Got it," they said together.

So much support in those two words. Paul appreciated it more than he could say. When the chips were down, the bullshit stopped and they were all one solid, united front.

He hurried to the studio, ready to go down on his knees and beg Ceci's forgiveness. Finding the place empty didn't help his rising panic. The chance he'd been hoping for this last year and he'd blown it.

Where the hell did she go? If she'd braved the paparazzi and left, that one guy Caz and Nick had seen would have been running for a shot, not trying to climb an elm tree. That meant she was still here.

Her bathroom. Of course—it was her own little corner of the house. She'd even mentioned them going there before they'd drifted off to sleep.

Paul spun around and rushed back into the house. He heard Caz and Nick's muffled voices coming from the den. His hopes deflated when he darted into the hallway and saw the door to Ceci's bathroom wide open and the room empty. Leaning against the wall, he tried to decide where to look next. That's when he noticed light under her closet door and the shadow indicating someone moved inside.

Ceci squeaked when he swung the door opened. She clutched fists full of pantyhose against her chest, her eyes wide, her cheeks flaming. God, she looked cute!

Paul smirked and braced his arms on the doorjamb. "What are you doing?"

She held up the pantyhose. "Seducing you?" Her red cheeks flushed all the more.

"With pantyhose? Were you going to put them on and parade around for me? Or did you intend for me to put them on for you?" He had to tease her. It was too good an opportunity not to do so. It wasn't often Ceci was caught at a loss for words.

She cocked her head to one side. "You'd put on pantyhose for me?"

"I'm not sure," he slowly replied. "Is that a trick question? A test of my love and devotion? Because I do love you and am completely devoted to you." He stepped into the closet with her and shut the door behind him. "After all, you're going to be the mother of my children."

Her smile dimmed the overhead light. "I am. I am going to be the mother of your children." Hose still fisted, she melted into his arms and met his lips.

He felt a tremor rattle through her and pulled up. "You're...nervous." He frowned. "Why?"

Another blush stained her cheeks. "I was going to try to t-tie you up."

"Really?" Blood rushed to his cock. He rubbed it over her stomach and brushed the backs of his fingers over her cheek and down her neck. Ceci shivered and arched her neck for more.

"And then what?" He traced his tongue around the shell of her ear, then lightly bit the lobe.

Her gasp rolled her pelvis over his erection, then she purposefully did it again. "You expect me to think when you're nibbling on me?"

"Then we're even. " He cupped her ass, holding her tight while he ground into her. "I can't think at all when I have your hot, perfect body against mine."

"Then I guess we'll have to let our actions speak louder than our words." She grazed her teeth over his Adam's apple, and all Paul could think about was having them playing with his balls.

"I'm at your mercy, sweetheart."

"Well, then…" She put him at arm's length. "Strip."

She didn't have to tell him twice. But then she dropped the hose and reached for the zipper on her dress. The barely-there rasp had the potency of nails slithered down his spine. Something hot and raw coiled at the base and spread to his groin. Paul tried for macho stud as he pulled his clothes off, but he had a strong feeling he came off as horny, drooling doofus. Ceci remained sleek and sexy, rivaling the most accomplished stripper. Her dress pooled at her feet, followed smoothly by bra and panties. Paul's jeans and shirt had been flung to the far corners of the huge closet.

"You look good enough to eat." Her voice caressed him seconds before she snagged a pair of hose and draped it around his neck.

"That's supposed to be my line." He cupped her breasts, pinching hard nipples between his thumbs and forefingers. Ceci's soft moan shot to his balls.

"Hands on the closet rods, big guy." She sawed the hose over his neck, then yanked it down and looped it around his erection. A slow rake nearly brought him to his knees.

It was a stretch to span the closet's width, so Paul wrapped his fingers around the rod on the right, leaving his manhood vulnerable to whatever she wanted to do. Ceci stabbed her beautiful breasts into his chest. Nipples scored lightning down his body as she stretched on tiptoes to reach one wrist. If he hadn't already come, he'd be spewing all over her.

"Not too tight, baby," he said as she knotted the hose around him. "It can slip and cut off circulation."

"Ah…you've done this before." She made the loop wider.

"No, just got a long lecture from Caz once on the proper bondage material and techniques when I dared suggest using pantyhose. He's takes his bondage very seriously."

Ceci scrunched her face. "Too much information."

He chuckled. "Sorry. Climb on board and I'll make it up to you."

Her eyes widened with her laugh. "Oh, my gosh! That's crazy. Think you can hold me?"

"I have a very strong penis." He wiggled his eyebrows and made his cock twitch.

She unsuccessfully fought a smirk and bound his other wrist. "Good. Because I wouldn't want to break it."

"That makes two of us," he quickly replied.

"Of course"—she drew her nails down his chest until they were wedged between them—"I could always kiss and make it better." She pinched his nipples with the tips of her nails and glided down his body.

Hot breath surrounded his cockhead. Ceci taunted him with the promise of her tongue, always a lick away from touching him. Paul tightened his grip on the closet rod. They were going for a fantasy here—he didn't want to destroy it from the start—and the pantyhose were token bondage. Though he swore waiting for her mouth would kill him, he let her have her moment, anticipating with each breath what she might do next and when she might do it. He closed his eyes and played the game, pretending to be at her mercy, while he tried to plan how he'd return the favor. His thoughts screeched to a halt when she sucked one of his balls into her mouth.

Paul groaned and thrust his hips forward. Fingernails tickled his ass, urging him to widen his stance. He did so, then stabbed his cock in the air, praying she'd suck it. She looped thumb and forefinger around the base, massaging the hard ridge underneath while she aimed her talented mouth for his other testicle.

He cried out and smacked his head on the closet rod. She released him and flashed her tongue behind his sac. Aiming for…

"Good God, baby!" She'd rimmed him! *Holy shit!*

Ragged gasps tore from his throat. She curled a loose fist around his cock and he humped it like a fiend, never quite getting the friction he needed, driving him crazy and making him love every second. Something cool and slick touched his rectum. Paul barely had time to process what it might be. A buzz alerted him too late. Without pause, she eased the dildo into him.

His body clenched from the invasion. He'd never…but damn it felt good! She worked it slowly in and out, taking it a little deeper each time. Vibrations rolled through his groin. Hot lips kneaded their way from the base of his erection all the way to the tip. She licked a circle around the crown, then sucked him deep.

Paul gritted his teeth against the rush, praying for the control to hang on just a little while longer. Praying not to come like a sixteen-year-old on his first fuck. Praying she'd never stop, that he could freeze this moment—

Ceci rubbed the dildo over his prostate. And he shot his load deep into her mouth…and just kept coming…and coming until the only thing holding him upright was the loose loops of pantyhose around his wrists. He slipped free, or maybe he fell. Paul was too dazed, too sweetly sated to notice. All he wanted was to touch her.

He felt her remove the toy and buried his fingers in her thick hair while she licked him clean. His legs couldn't hold him, but he managed to crumble to the floor in a controlled manner, arms surrounding her as he drew her up to kiss her.

Talk about freezing a moment. He wanted to propose that very minute, sweep her off to the nearest place they could find and marry her so they wouldn't waste one more second of life together. But Paul also wanted her to know his proposal was sincere, not given in the heat of the moment or the rush of the afterglow.

Should he dare? After all, she was going to be the mother of his children.

He broke off the kiss at the thought and smiled. She beamed with love, adoration. If he didn't know better, he would have said she was the one who'd just had the body-quaking orgasm instead of him. If he'd been able to get it up at that second, Paul would have taken care of that little inconsistency…and taken the first step toward those children.

"You know…" He weighed her breast in his palm, drawing lazy circles over the hard tip. "I was supposed to be doing all that to you."

Ceci wrapped her leg around his calf. “There’s always later.”

“Sorry for the turnaround period, sweetheart, but you literally drained me.” He gave her nipple a tweak. “Won’t you join me in bliss?”

Her giggle faded into a gasp when he pinched a little harder. She tightened her hold around his leg and rubbed her crotch over his flaccid penis. Paul damned his need to recharge. The only thing he wanted more than to fuck her was to please her, make her come in his arms.

Paul pulled upright and spooned her into the cove of his body. She rested her head on his shoulder with a contented sigh. Emotion he’d withheld for too long choked him.

“I love you, Ceci. I love you so much. And I’m going to spend the rest of our lives showing you just how much.”

He slid his fingers down her body and into her sopping pussy.

*   *   *

Goose bumps peppered Ceci’s skin in the wake of Paul’s fingers. She loved the feel of his solid body behind her, his muscular arms protecting her from the world, his callused-roughened touch igniting fires that demanded to be quenched. She hadn’t intended to do all this in the closet, but she was oh-so-glad she had. This was decadently erotic.

She lifted her knees and let them open. Paul slid his legs beneath hers and lifted, spreading her wider. No hose held her in place, but she felt bound just the same. Open to him to take what he wanted, when he wanted, how he wanted.

Her clit strained for his touch. Paul slid his fingers down the sides, deep into her valleys until the hard nub was scissored between his fingers. He pinched it lightly, the slick juices making it evasive. He smeared more over it, circling with the same precision he plucked those guitar strings.

Ceci writhed against him, hand clutching his neck, digging into his soft hair. He whispered her name, then latched onto an extra-sensitive tendon below her ear. Lips kneaded her hard, forcing one gasp after the other from her. Her eyes rolled back in her head. She closed her eyes and groaned, rolling her hips higher into his hand.

He stabbed his fingers into her pussy, pumping deep and high. Instinct clenched her thighs, trying to lock his hand in place. His knees kept them apart and his to play with. She whimpered in frustration and tried to lift her hips. A hard pinch to her nipple froze her…and doubled her agony.

"Where's your little toy?" His voice rumbled against her ear, setting tremors through her body.

"Over there." Ceci couldn't point to save her life.

"You used a condom over it, right?"

"Yes," she managed to reply.

"I'm not going to do that with you now. Get it. You're pussy is so wet…I can tell it craves everything I can give it." The words whispered through her.

She couldn't answer, could only fumble for the small dildo. Her hand shook when she gave it to Paul. "I've never…"

"Neither had I until you, sweetheart." He wrapped his hand around it, then nudged it against her anus. "You took my virginity. It's only fair…"

A gentle push eased it inside, beyond the tight muscle. Waves of pleasure rolled over her like nothing she'd ever imagined. He pressed the heel of his hand against her clit and she ground into it. Each plunge brought more sensation; contractions built from deep inside, pooling outward.

"This is how I'm going to fuck you there, baby." His voice, so deep, a melody for her alone. "Slow and steady."

Ceci snapped one hand over his forearm, the other grappled his neck. "Oh, God… I can't believe it. I coming," she gasped. "I'm already—"

"Yes, baby…come."

The words carried her over the top. Orgasm poured from her in rolling undulations, harder than she'd ever dreamed possible. She collapsed into him, barely aware of him removing the toy, only feeling when his arms and legs surrounded her. Sweet kisses helped cushion her descent back to earth.

"I sure could use that bubble bath right now." She sounded lazy, sated…well loved.

"Now that sounds like the perfect plan." He squeezed a hug around her. "Of course, that means we have to move."

"Soon as my liquefied muscles return to normal," she said with a small laugh.

"I sure know that feeling." He chuckled. "Ceci, I—"

A rap at the closet door intruded. He and Ceci didn't budge.

"Yeah?" he called out.

"Conference call in fifteen minutes," Nick said. "Ducks in a row, circling the wagons, and all that shit." He paused, then added, "Sorry."

Disappointment sighed through both of them.

"Go…you need to take care of your family." She brushed her arms over his.

Paul traced the curve of her cheek. "*You* are my family. The sooner I can do two things, the happier I'll be."

She brushed her nose over his. "And what might those two things be?"

"Make love to you in a proper bed…and marry you. I love you, Ceci. I love you so much. Marry me. Now. No more delays."

"Oh, absolutely." She slid her arms over his and tightened them around her. "Think we can sneak out under the cover of the paparazzi?"

"I think we can give it a damn good try."

"Guys, I need an answer," Nick said. "Now."

"Pull your panties out of your crack," Paul said, and Ceci buried her snicker in the curve of his neck. "We're coming."

"Yeah, well, we don't have time to wait for the two of you to come again."

"Smart ass," Ceci tossed out.

"You can't blame me," Nick replied. "The bedrooms might be soundproof, but the closet sure as hell isn't and you two have got me and Caz climbing the walls. Get a room, for cryin' out loud. Conference call…*thirteen* minutes."

"I'll be there," Paul replied, then smiled. "Actually, I'll take it in the bathroom."

EPILOGUE

Another shocker from Mesquite. What next?

And another heartbreaker for all you ladies out there. Wedding bells are ringing for—get this—Paul Tristan and Ceci Powers. Seems Ceci and our sweet-voiced Pablo have been eyeing each other from the start. So does that mean Brian's relationship with Ceci was a ruse to protect his wife and child? We may never know with this close-knit, tight-lipped band of brothers.

No word yet on when they'll wed. Sources suspect it will be right away since the couple have indicated they'd like to start a family soon. Chances are they'll wait until the dust settles from the termination of long-time manager, Howard Ramsey.

Who'll replace Howie is anyone's guess, but it's speculated that record company execs are pushing go-getter Brooke Hansen to the forefront, a move both Mesquite's attorney and agent both support. Reports say the major stumbling block in signing her on is getting Casper Tristan's approval. The two have butted heads on more than one occasion. We doubt very seriously if this will wind up being a ruse of any kind. If looks could kill, these two would have done each other in a long time ago.

Who'll hold the managerial reins for our superstars? Not Brooke. Not if Caz can help it. Will he cave to his brothers? It might just be the deal breaker for these all-for-one brothers. We'll keep you posted.

IF LOOKS COULD KILL

CHAPTER 1

Brooke Hansen tightened her grip on her black leather tote, kept her gaze locked on the towering building before her, and kept walking. *They* followed every step—entertainment reporters, paparazzi, fans. Thousands of questions slammed her way, so many, so fast, and from so many sources, it all became one big, unintelligible buzz. Not responding, not being rude took discipline Brooke never expected to have to exercise in the workplace. All she wanted to do was tell them all to fuck off. She was nervous enough without having to account for her every move and action.

She stared at the skyscraper, focusing on the black glass that mirrored the circus around her. Entertainment reporters swallowed microphones. Paparazzi waved cameras from every possible position. And above it all were the banners and posters: *Mesquite 4-Ever, We Love You, Marry Me, Have MY Baby.* Band members' names were interchanged—Brian, Paul aka Pablo, Caz, or Nick—but the message was the same everywhere. Brooke just didn't need the reminder right now of how very important this deal was to her career, her well-being, the goals she'd set.

Traffic had made her late for the biggest meeting of her life. These *people* blocking her access were making her even later. She was going to be fired before she officially started working for her dream clients. At least she'd been able to call in and let them know she was unavoidably running late.

Managing rock band Mesquite had been on her wish list for years.

With Howard Ramsey's abrupt dismissal, that goal became reality…after she'd just about begged her company to assign her. That was the easy part. Getting Mesquite to agree to hire her wasn't. Brooke knew without asking which Tristan brother objected—Caz. They'd butted heads on more than one occasion. He made no bones about the fact he considered her pushy and aggressive. She, in turn, found him to be the scariest person she'd ever met.

Brooke's heart raced. She swallowed past the lump in her throat and tried not to run in to the revolving doors just ahead. Her reflection beckoned her in to safety. She double-checked her appearance, praising her red power suit, cursing the tendrils of dark hair that refused the confines of her up-do. She looked like she'd just stepped out of a hot tub and threw on a suit. Like the Universe mocked her attempt to look professional, reminding Brooke she was way out of her league with Mesquite.

She stepped into the revolving door, leaving her followers behind. *Not too late to turn back. Just keep walking and come back out.*

Damn, she hated threshold guardians. She walked into the lobby and on to the bank of elevators before she could give in to the fear, turn tail and run. Polished doors opened upon her approach. She didn't have to pause. Once inside the elevator, the doors closed her in silence.

"It *is* too late," she told herself as she pressed the button for the twelfth floor. "I have my reputation, my pride, my goals." And if she didn't carry this through, she'd regret it for the rest of her life. Getting Mesquite as her clients, even though she still worked for Catalina Entertainment, was a major step in her goal to strike out on her own.

As the floors dinged past her, Brooke tried to sweep the errant strands of hair up. They refused to tuck into place and time was too short to dash to the nearest ladies room to fix it. *Nothing to be done about it now.* Or the sweat that soaked the lining of her suit. Or the heartbeat that ran circles around the elevator, then raced ahead of her once the doors opened.

The receptionist guarding the inner sanctum of the law office lifted her gnome-like head, her wizened features narrowing in on Brooke. She half-expected the ageless woman to demand a password before she could go any farther. Brooke could see the condemnation in the woman's cold blue eyes—*You're late, missy. Go right to the principal's office. No soup for you. Not by the hair of my chinny-chin-chin.* And a thousand other phrases to make Brooke run screaming back to her fairy-tale world, because her goals were nothing more than the dust of dreams. Too far-fetched to be realized.

She preferred the bubbly Amazon who guarded the portal to her brother's law office—welcoming, yet clearly capable of taking down an intruder with one look. Reid's law firm was new, bright, cutting edge; Marvin Keating's evoked old and well-established. The two men had much more in common than most people realized. Both had help guide Brooke in her career and personal life.

"Ms. Hansen I presume?" *Who's that nibbling on my house?*

Brooke hauled her bravado from the depths of her quivering soul. "Correct."

"They're in the conference room waiting. I'll let them know you've finally arrived, then escort you." *Come into my den, little fly.*

"Not necessary." She used the crisp tone so effective in dealing with her own staff. "I'm sure you have better things to do than walk with me."

"Indeed." Her gnarled fingers lifted the phone in slow motion and pressed the intercom. "Ms. Hansen has arrived, Mr. Keating. Yes, sir." She lifted her nose toward Brooke as she hung up. "Third door on your left." She dismissed her with a jerk of her head and returned to sorting the stack of mail before her.

Brooke's heels clicked on the glossy floor. Anyone listening would hear her coming. She prayed she didn't lose her footing on the slick tile. That indignity might be the straw forcing her to run the other way. Ahead, a door opened on the designated room. Marvin Keating stuck his head out. His bright smile greeted her, but did little to calm her nerves. She still appreciated the effort. No wonder the ladies—and more than a few men—called him a silver fox. He could definitely turn on the charm when he wanted. He also had the bite of a shark. Brooke appreciated that, too. No nonsense whatsoever. The man did the job required of him and then some. His discretion in all matters, personal and business, was unquestionable.

"Glad you were as close as you were when that accident on the 405 backed up all the freeways," he said, extending his hand to shake hers.

"That makes two of us." She clasped his hand and gave a small laugh. There was power in the firm, brief handshake. The look in Marvin's eyes telegraphed support and a silent, *Don't let them see you sweat.* Brooke added a quick nod, *Message received,* and they dropped hands.

He waved her across the threshold, and Brooke stepped into a dark-paneled conference room that screamed money. Table polished to a high sheen, carafes of coffee, pitchers of ice water, legal pads with Waterman pens and dark green folders stacked at every seat, brown leather captain chairs around the table, state of the art audiovisual equipment on the far wall. The look alone intimidated her. It always did but more so today when her career and dreams were depending on what happened next. The sight of the six men, who stood when she entered, chased away any remaining doubt that this was the big time.

Her heartbeat tripled. The Tristan brothers—Mesquite—all hers...if she didn't blow it. Brooke passed a quick gaze over them, always amazed at how closely they resembled each other. It was the brown hair and eyes that gave the illusion of similarity. Each was markedly different in looks and personality once one looked beyond the initial glance. She'd known them for a while. In the business, everyone "knew" everyone else. She'd had drinks with Nick once and a few times with Brian and Paul. And Caz?

Caz scared her half to death. He'd made it clear the more distance between them the better and, for the most part, Brooke was happy to oblige. But now it was business. And one thing Brooke had learned very early in her career was if you wanted to play with the big boys, a woman had to show she had balls as big as or bigger than theirs.

More handshakes went around the room. Three brothers added a "Hi" and a smile; Caz merely grunted at her. Brooke forced herself to meet his glower with a smile, but quickly shifted to their agent, Chuck Skinner. The big surprise was seeing Mac Manus. She'd known someone from the record company would attend. She just didn't anticipate it would be the man in charge. Definitely a make-or-break moment. A lot of money was on the line. She could not fuck this up.

Brooke was going to be the liaison between Mesquite and the other men gathered here. There was no better time to start than right now. She visualized wrapping her hand around the reins of control and took charge. "Shall we begin, gentlemen?"

She slipped into the only vacant chair, pulling her files from her black leather tote as she did so. The men did so as well, adjusting writing tablets and folders for use during the meeting.

She could feel Caz's gaze boring a hole through her from the opposite side of the table. His glare unnerved her as it always did. Brooke always had a hard time looking him in the eye. If they were going to work together, she had to get over that. She ordered her folders and forced her gaze up to his. He didn't blink. His only movement was the pen he drummed against the legal pad. She'd watched his precision in concert over the years, working those drums with the flick of his wrist. She'd never realized until now how strong his arms were. Brooke could see the muscles flex with every move. Each pen thump against the paper echoed her heartbeat. She quelled the shiver that threatened to overcome her, pulled in a breath, and glanced around the table at the others.

"I need to know the circumstances behind Howard Ramsay's dismissal." Ramsay had been with Mesquite from the beginning. Despite pressure from the record company, agent, and lawyer, Ramsay had remained…until now. Something big had happened and, in order to represent Mesquite fully, Brooke needed all information to be prepared to address accusations, assumptions, and fallout.

Brian Tristan laced his fingers on the table and leaned forward, gaze locked to hers. "He lied and manipulated events to keep me from my wife and child."

She frowned, but maintained eye contact. "Why?"

"Money."

Ah, yes, the all-mighty dollar. Brooke didn't interrupt as Brian briefed on her the extent of Ramsey's intrusion—keeping Brian and Lexy Claremont from each other with lies built on their fears, taking advantage of their youth, never once informing Brian he had a son. The man was fortunate one of the Tristans hadn't threatened to cut off his balls, but then that would have involved making a threat, and these men were very careful about the image they cultivated.

"I have a team reviewing all the contracts Ramsey had with Mesquite, searching for any breaches within," Marvin Keating said. "If we can find those, we might be able to see he gets no further cut from Mesquite's past royalties and merchandising…anything negotiated during his term."

"Good." She made a quick note of that. Though she trusted Marvin implicitly, Brooke liked to stay on top of things. Who knew what else Howie had kept from Mesquite over the years? But, with Marvin's team on the case, she knew they'd damn sure find out.

"We've also discussed a possible lawsuit," he added.

Brooke slowly shook her head. "To what end? Mesquite doesn't need the money. Yes, the money awarded could go to charity and that would be a very nice thing. However, is the publicity and time consumed in taking Ramsey to court worth it? I know it's rough now with the paparazzi, but it'll get worse with a lawsuit.

"There'll be enough of an adjustment period for Brian, Lexy, and

Ethan without having to worry about court appearances and such. Let it go. Men like Ramsey will get their comeuppance one day. I doubt anyone, anywhere will hire him again. Word filtering to our company indicates he's lost more clients since his dismissal by Mesquite. He'll get his and it'll do him a lot more damage in the long run. I say save the time and energy for your family."

Brian leaned back, the hint of a smile dancing on his lips. She wished she could gauge Marvin's reaction, not that she cared if she'd pissed him off. Brooke had a job to do and she knew her logic was sound. The decision was ultimately the brothers'.

"What's the situation with Ceci Powers?" She focused attention on Paul Tristan. "I know what the media is saying, but I'd like to hear it directly from you."

Paul's position was a mirror image of Brian's—the hint of a smile, chin resting on the points of his fingers, kicked back in the chair, elbow on the armrest. "We're getting married as soon as we can. No, her relationship with Brian wasn't a ruse, but it was short-lived. She and I just finally saw the light."

She cocked her head toward Brian. "And you're good with that?"

"Very good." His smile widened. "Ceci's a great person. I'm thrilled she and Paul are together."

Chuck Skinner cleared his voice. "I thought a photo spread in *People* would be good. They're willing to pay a pretty penny for the rights. All proceeds will go to charity. We'll call it 'Heartbreakers' and have Brian and Paul at home with their ladies—"

"No." Brooke didn't hesitate to cut him off. She'd never heard of a worse idea. Judging from the glower on his face, she did need to smooth some feathers. "Mesquite has always been a united force. All the brothers standing together and against the vagaries of the world. To do a shoot on two brothers and their wives smacks of division. 'United We Stand, Divided We Fall.' Mesquite's strength comes from their solidarity. We don't want to screw with that. Now if all four brothers had wives or fiancées…"

She slid her gaze Nick and Caz's way. Nick shrugged and shook his head. Caz? Those eyes again…that unwavering gaze that stripped Brooke of her soul. She fought the need to look away. This was a battle of wills, and she would prevail.

"I suppose you're going to nix the *Dancing With The Stars* gig," Nick said.

Brooke snapped her head his way. "Please tell me you're joking."

"And if he isn't?" Each word from Caz was slow, deliberate, and deep-toned. She felt the rumble of it deep inside. It stole her breath, made her want to clutch the collar of her suit jacket to her throat and run far, far away.

"Then I would question why. Are we talking performing as a group? Not too bad a move if you weren't presently sky-lined. Ditto with performing on *Saturday Night Live*. Don't get me wrong. I love the show, but I have to advise on what's best for Mesquite. If this was a normal circumstance, I might agree, even though the show's focus is on the dancers, not the entertainment showcased. But I certainly wouldn't agree to doing so with the recent…upheaval. Message board posters can be merciless in their criticism. They could find flaw where none exists, simply because of what's happened in your personal lives. Once they attack you one place, they'll go for the throat and rehash the personal situation, too. You have enough adverse publicity surrounding you without dredging up more. Plus, such an appearance could very well seem to smack of PR-spin and damage control. None of you have anything to hide, so why make it seem like you're going on the defensive? Unless there's something I don't know about."

Caz's lips thinned. Brooke couldn't tell if there was fire or ice in the look he gave her. Her pounding heart filled the silence.

He eased back with a smirk. "I'm an open book, baby."

Baby? Uh-uh. Brooke spread her fingers on the shiny tabletop. "With all due respect, *Mr.* Tristan, I am a professional businesswoman, not 'baby' or 'honey' or whatever other endearment might be floating around in your head."

"My apologies." His scathing tone indicated otherwise. "I thought baby was much more preferable than bitch."

Someone's gasp sucked the air out of the room. Brooke ignored it. She knew coming into this that she and Caz were going to butt heads. Better to get it out in the open now. "My name is Brooke or Ms. Hansen. Please use one or the other."

"That was uncalled for, Caz," Paul told his brother.

"Was it?" Those piercing dark eyes raked over her face and downward. "She arrives late, then sits down and immediately starts telling us what to do. What would you call it?"

"Doing her job?" Brian replied.

"And with some very good insight and thought." Nick braced his forearms on the table. "Back to the *Dancing With The Stars* gig…"

Caz snorted.

Nick ignored him. "If one of us were going to compete…"

Brooke shook inside, but forced order into her thoughts, forced herself not to climb over the table and strangle Caz. "Again, I would question why. It's a great venue for getting your name out there, great career boost. Are you trying for more endorsements? Are you trying to expand your individual career into a different arena? Competing means only one of you is highlighted and there goes your all-for-one image. Which leads me to ask…why in the world did you buy a house together? In my opinion, that's carrying togetherness a bit too far."

"Tell us about it," Brian, Paul, and Nick said at the same time, then laughed.

"We were advised to invest in real estate," Brian told her.

"And the recording studio in the back made it too tempting to resist," Nick added. "We were together all the time, so we thought it would save us time and hassle."

"But even we agree it's too much," Paul said. "Ceci and I love the house and are buying the other three out. Brian and Lexy are looking to buy locally and will move once Ethan's current school year is finished. Nick and Caz are searching."

Caz leaned her way. Despite the width of the table between them, Brooke felt like he hovered over her. Heat raced through her veins, doubling her heart rate.

"And what advice would you have had regarding real estate investment?" he asked.

Think. Think. Brooke moistened her dry lips. His gaze locked onto her mouth, then slid to her eyes slowly. *The big bad wolf in all his glory.*

"Everyone needs a place to live, so buying a home isn't off the charts crazy. I might also suggest the four of you consider a production company." She glanced at Manus, realizing she'd just fucked up.

"Not music, of course," she quickly said. "I'm thinking movies and television. Consider diversification, too. Put your eggs in other baskets. Make your money work for you. Planning for the future is crucial in entertainment. Also…" She pulled in yet another breath to steady her nerves. "There's been mention twice today of donations to charitable organizations. Very admirable. I would suggest, however, you start your own foundation."

"Ceci would love to do something like that," Paul said.

From the corner of her eye, Brooke saw him making notes.

Caz eased into his seat and parked his chin on the tips of his long fingers. All Brooke could see was those fingers fisted in her hair, him yanking her close enough to devour. The image and thoughts it bred unsettled her.

"I love your ideas," Nick said. "Paul's right. Ceci could really sink her teeth into something like this. I think we're going to work great together. And I, for one, am thrilled we've hired you."

Brian and Paul quickly concurred.

Caz continued his predatory glare. "I'm clearly outnumbered here, but I will concede the point that your ideas have great merit."

"Thank you." Brooke wasn't above a glare of her own. She prayed it came off icy and not I'm-scared-to-death. "Perhaps there's hope as we continue to work together that you and I will find common ground upon which to co-exist."

"Perhaps." He tilted a nod her way.

Nick scuffed his hands together. "What else do you have in mind?"

Brooke flipped open her notepad and continued. She was in. Now she had to make sure she stayed there.

"Gentlemen, it's time to re-energize. To not only look outside the box, but also at what's been hiding in the corners."

CHAPTER 2

She'd certainly passed all their tests with flying colors, Caz would give her that much. It still didn't change his opinion that she was a ball-busting bitch. He'd met linebackers who were less aggressive than Brooke Hansen was. Grown men crouched at her feet quivering from the force. And yet Caz had never once heard of or seen her lose her temper, much less raise her voice. Firm? Yes. Sarcastic? Oh yes. This was a woman who spoke her mind, who got the job done, who fought like a she-wolf for her clients. In other words, she was perfect for Mesquite.

Caz wanted her gone.

Brooke threatened his control and had from the minute he'd first met her. An instant of time that haunted his nights, fucked with his head, and generally made him a stranger to himself. He'd thought her eyes were black, then realized later that they were midnight blue, the perfect match to her black hair, both accentuated by a creamy complexion models craved. Even the sun didn't dare to mar her skin.

From first glance, Caz had wanted to stab his hand in her hair and yank it free. He couldn't stand not knowing how long it was. He'd wanted to fuck with her control the way she'd fucked with his. Undoing the French twist seemed like a good start. Which made the tendrils escaping the hairstyle now way too distracting. The coal-black strands curled down her neck, over her temple to kiss her ear, behind the lobe and forward. Not once had she tried to shove them into place. Her long, French-manicured nails focused exclusively on the folders and work before her. Nothing penetrated her work mantle. How could those strands of hair not bother her? They sure as hell bothered him.

Caz wanted to stretch across the table and thrust his finger into one of those wayward curls, feel it wrap around his finger, see if it was really as soft as it looked. That's how she'd trap him. Hair clinging like ivy to him, drawing him into her like a Venus flytrap. She'd wrest control from him with nothing more than a glance and perhaps one of those barely perceptible sighs that yanked his attention to the breasts locked behind the armor of her suits.

She'd drop him before her to feast upon, leaving him a dry husk of a man craving her juices for sustenance, then she'd plunge her high heel into his heart as she walked over him in her quest for new prey. Caz squirmed in his seat, trying without success to adjust the erection straining the seams in his trousers. He wanted her on her knees, midnight blue eyes staring up at him through those impossibly long lashes, waiting for his command. Naked with moon glow revealing the blush on her skin from a soft flogger. He'd order her hair unbound, demand she keep her hard nipples upthrust as she did so. If she disobeyed, he'd clamp the little beads; yank them tight on a golden leash. Show her who was in charge. Hurt her before she could hurt him.

Caz blinked the scenario away. This is what frightened him—the loss of control. As a top, he prided himself on caring for those who placed their trust in him. Not once had he violated that trust. But Brooke's control usurped his and all Caz had wanted was to wrest it away from her by any and all means at his disposal. He avoided her like the plague. It was the only way to clear his head and put order back into his life.

The Universe had a wicked sense of humor, though, throwing her right in his path where he couldn't ignore her. He'd been in agony since his brothers voted to bring her on board. Caz felt the walls closing in every waking minute of the day. It was worse at night when no one else was around to help occupy his wayward thoughts…except Brooke. Caz took his frustration out on his drums or the keyboard…or his cock. His sour mood filtered over to other things. And just when he thought he had it all locked on, she walked in the door.

Her lateness alternately pleased and pissed him off—*so she's human after all; how dare she keep us waiting.* Then she breezed past Marvin with a bright smile, glowing eyes, and hair looking like she'd tumbled out of someone's arms. Probably leaving the poor guy as frustrated as Caz.

He could smell her perfume—a whiff of something citrusy—as she shook his hand, then sat across from him, giving him an unintentional shot of cleavage. His gaze had wandered to the spot, hoping for another glimpse. Nick's knee nudge reminded Caz of his manners, but by that time Caz was way beyond polite. He wanted more than the tease of perfume. He wanted to crawl under the table, shove up her little red skirt, and wedge his face in her crotch. Let her *try* to keep her composure under the onslaught of his tongue.

She allowed him momentary victory when she slid her gaze away from him and toward the table. Before he could bask in the glory, however, those dark blue eyes locked back on him, daring him to be the first to blink. A cattle prod up the ass would have had less impact. His balls felt the burn in her eyes, yet she had the nerve to sit there, calm and cool, as if nothing had passed between them.

Now she wouldn't look at him at all. He'd been "dismissed" as she outlined ideas and plans. Oh, she'd spare him a glance from time to time, but Caz knew it was more of an afterthought to ensure he wasn't "left out." Rage boiled inside him. More conflicting emotion warred inside his head.

One minute he wanted to grab the back of her neck and force her to look at him and him alone, see him as a man, *her* man, right before he plundered her mouth in a kiss her clit would feel. The next minute he wanted to step behind her, massage the tension from her shoulders, run his hands down her suit jacket, open those buttons, and cup the treasure guarded within. Her breasts would surge into his hands. He'd nibble her neck, tease the nipples, and show her a pleasure like none she'd known before.

He wanted her at his feet, then he found himself wanting to be at hers. Agony spawned a killer headache and threatened to split his cock in two. How in the hell was he supposed to survive working with this woman? He had to get back some measure of control, had to purge her from his system and his head, once and for all.

"Caz?"

He blinked himself into the here and now at the sound of Nick's voice. Everyone was looking at him. He was obviously supposed to answer some question. It would have been nice if he knew what. Caz wasn't about to let Brooke know he'd been distracted.

"Sounds good to me," he said. His brothers would vote him down no matter what at this point. He might as well agree upfront and save one argument.

Judging from everyone's puzzled looks, however, Caz suspected his response revealed he didn't have a clue what was being discussed. He braced himself for Brooke's sarcastic retort regarding his inattention. Instead, with a flick of her finger, she closed the folder before her.

"Excellent." The portfolio was next.

The others started closing files, too. What the hell had he agreed to?

Marvin pushed his chair away from the table. "I've sent a letter to Howie demanding any and all files, documents, and correspondence regarding Mesquite be turned over to my office by close of business tomorrow. I'll forward you a copy of that this afternoon."

"Wonderful." Brooke turned a smile toward their agent. "Chuck, if you could email me the schedule of appearances and such, that would be great. I can juggle better when I have all the balls."

A different image clenched Caz's sac—his testicles perched on the tips of her nails.

"And we'll send over a status check on where we are on the new album," Brian added.

"Any rough cuts for me to listen to? Any chance of sitting in on a session?" she asked.

Paul tsked. "We really prefer to smooth out songs before letting anyone hear them. We've discovered it really screws with our creative process to share stuff before we're satisfied with it."

"Understood." She gave a nod. "But my intent is not to be critical or tell you how to write your songs. What I'd like to have is a good understanding of your particular creative process. The more familiar I am with all of you, the better I'll be able to manage. My goal is to be your right hand, your liaison, your gatekeeper, as it were. I definitely don't want to be up your asses."

Fuck! Caz shoved away from the table. "Sorry, something I ate." Oral sex supplanted anal sex in his overloaded brain. *No, no, no!* He dashed from the room, each step more painful than the last as his erection threatened to erupt.

Once the door sighed shut behind him, Caz glanced up and down the vacant corridor to ensure he was alone before he grabbed the log of a hard-on and yanked it into a more comfortable position. His penis surged with the touch, balls tight against his body and just as ready to come as the rest of him. The nearest restroom felt like it was miles away instead of two doors down. He hoped he could make it.

Caz couldn't believe he'd been reduced to this—beating off in a public bathroom. But he couldn't bear the pressure a second longer.

Wedged behind his fly, his cock protested confinement even as it gloried in the rub of twill over its length. Caz didn't hesitate when he reached his goal. Quick strides carried him to the last stall. He prayed no one else was in there. At this point, he couldn't bend down to look without fear he'd snap his penis in two.

He shut and latched the door, then leaned against it and released the beast. His dick surged to freedom. He fumbled for a wad of toilet paper and pressed it to the crown with barely enough time to spare. In fewer than ten strokes he was coming. He'd had more stamina as a teenager. So much for control; he couldn't even control this but, God, the relief was sweet. And there was no one to witness his lapse except his ego.

Tension drifted away on post-orgasmic bliss. His legs threatened to give out, muscles now jellied instead of steel-hard. He didn't have the luxury of basking in the after-glow. Any minute now one of his brothers would hunt him down, demanding an explanation for his behavior. The confrontation was inevitable and, honestly, he deserved being chewed out. Caz preferred it be on his own turf rather than that of their attorney.

He flushed and tucked and was washing his hands when Marvin Keating strolled in. The lawyer didn't bother with the ruse of having to pee. He walked right up to Caz and leaned into the wall.

"You're overly tense." His tone suggested a conversation as innocent as discussing the weather. "Your control is slipping. Being on the road as long as you were has taken its toll. I'm having a gathering tonight. Why don't you and Nick come? There'll be new faces, a scene you might be interested in. In fact, it has your names written all over it."

Caz met his gaze in the mirror. The man knew him well. "Thanks, Marvin. We'll be there."

Marvin clasped his shoulder, gave it a squeeze and a pat, then left.

Amazing how that little invite calmed Caz. It was exactly what he needed. He'd be able to get through the rest of the meeting knowing he'd could re-center himself tonight. But when he exited the restroom, he found Nick lounging against the wall, fingertips tucked in his trouser pockets while he waited for Caz.

"Meeting's over," he said. "Brian and Paul walked out with the others. They'll be in the car."

Caz presumed that meant Brooke, too. Disappointment weighed him down. He'd been looking forward to showing her nothing she said or did would bother him. Now he felt like she'd dismissed him, like he wasn't worth her time or energy. It grated against his nerves. Caz wanted to run after her and show her who was really in charge. Shove her against the nearest wall, lift her skirt, and give her something to think about the rest of the afternoon.

His balls clenched at the thought of being buried inside her. Imagined moans and pleas for *more, more, more* ran through his head. She'd squeeze him tight when she came, but he'd hold out, fucking her all the harder until the only thing holding her upright was the cock nailing her to the wall.

"You were out of line in there," Nick said, cutting through Caz's red haze.

In full defensive mode, he frowned at his little brother. "You know how I feel about her."

Nick smirked. "Yes, that's more than apparent." He glanced down at Caz's bulging crotch, then back up. "To everyone when you made your mad dash to the head."

Heat rushed up his neck, and there wasn't a damn thing he could do about it. She had an edge on him now. How long before she used it to her advantage? Or could he use it to his? To throw her off? To keep her in line?

Caz hated where his thoughts carried him. There was more at stake here than his stupid pride. This was about their careers and that was something he couldn't fuck with. He truly was out of control and out of line. But he'd be damned if he'd apologize to Brooke. The best he could offer was to move on from here.

"It won't happen again. I've got it under control. Let's just go." He walked away, Nick right behind him. Caz braced himself for a bigger lecture, but Nick said nothing more on the subject, or anything else for that matter. It made waiting for the elevator awkward. Finally, Caz broke the silence.

"Marvin invited us to a gathering tonight. Says he has a new scene we might enjoy."

"I sincerely hope you have yourself reined in by then. The last thing you need right now is to have *that* reputation in the toilet. Everyone in the community will shut you out. Instead of having your name whispered with awe and respect, it'll be snickered, snorted, and sneered."

Caz rolled his gaze toward the suspended ceiling tiles. "Good God, you're dramatic."

Nick lifted his palms. "Just trying to make a point and get it through that thick head of yours." He jabbed a finger toward Caz's erection. "Both of them."

Caz frowned at his brother. "I'll worry about my own cock, thank you very much. I'll handle it. This is my problem and no one else's."

"Yes, we're all aware of how you handled it. And you made it everyone else's problem when you waved the thing in front of everyone's eyes when you fell over yourself to leave the meeting."

Now Nick was just pissing him off. "The invitation was for both of us. Are you going with me or not?"

"I'm going. Someone needs to keep you in check." Nick stepped into the elevator the minute the doors open.

"Or disown me if I fuck up?" Caz snapped back.

Nick grinned. "Something like that."

Caz joined him and punched the button for the lobby. "What happened to all-for-one?"

His brother snorted. "You sorta blew that out of the water in the meeting, Casper. It was more than clear we weren't united. Thank God we were behind closed doors in a relatively safe environment. Suck it up and slap a smile on when we're in public. Brooke is the best, and we've got her. You heard her ideas. Oh…wait…no, you didn't. You were too busy checking out her tits and praying for a boob shot."

Caz watched his face flame in the elevator's mirrored walls. Since he couldn't dispute the accusation, he kept his mouth shut. Thankfully, his silence also bought Nick's. They stood side by side, right hand clasped over left wrist on the ride down, Nick's gaze still continuing to judge Caz in their reflections. It was the longest elevator ride of his life. When the doors sighed open on the lobby, he let Nick take the forefront, but only allowed him to put a half step between them. Paul and Brian exchanged a last round of handshakes with their agent. Everyone had already left. Beyond the revolving glass door, reporters milled about and fans hovered behind them waving their signs. All crowded Chuck when the door spit him onto the street. The man merely smiled, lifted a wave, and pushed his way through to the parking garage across the street where a knot of reporters had Mac cornered.

Foolish people. He'll eat them for lunch.

"Did Brooke make it out okay?" he asked. There was no time better than now to try to mend bridges with his brothers.

"She's still with Marvin," Brian said. "They had other business to discuss. But I wouldn't worry about Brooke, if I were you. She's hell on wheels, has a great head on her shoulders, and has certainly more than proven she can soar above the greatest of adversities."

The last word came with a pointed look from Brian that Caz had no trouble interpreting. "Yeah, I get it. I fucked up," he snapped. "Discussion closed. It won't happen again." He shifted a glance Paul's way. "And make sure Ceci knows that I've already been lectured and don't want to hear it again."

Caz started to march away, then jerked to a stop. United…the face Mesquite had to show to the world. Pulling in a breath, he squared his shoulders and returned to them. No one called him on it, thank God. Reporters swamped them the second Mesquite cleared the revolving door and allowed Chuck and Mac clean getaways.

Caz and his brothers ran the gauntlet as they always did—smile, wave, keep walking. Not once during the drive home did the guys say a word to him. That was fine with Caz. The last thing he needed was more lecturing. He knew he deserved their anger—enough said. He was plenty pissed at himself. Tonight he'd get his control locked on and his actions today would be history. That hope kept him sane, but it did little to keep his mind off Brooke Hansen.

Caz mulled over his obsession with her during the drive home. He stared at the passing scenery without seeing it. He relived every word and action from the meeting. Dissected the few interactions he'd had with her before today. In each instance, it felt like she'd crawled under his skin and taken over his brain. Tension like nothing he'd ever experienced locked his muscles. A long soak in the hot tub would calm him, but he doubted he'd have the privacy that normally went with it.

Brian's wife and son had arrived with Brian last night to meet the family. They'd bonded instantly with their parents and Ceci. Essentially they'd taken over the house—in a good way, of course. Plans for Ceci and Paul's wedding overlapped holiday plans, decorating plans, plans for plans that made Caz's head swim with how quickly the conversation shifted. The place needed to be filled with laughter and fun. Once they all heard how he'd behaved today…

So much for no more lecturing. It was only a question of who would take a bigger chunk of his ass—Ceci or his mother. Caz didn't want to deal with it. The minute Paul pulled into the garage of their Hollywood Hills home, Caz shouldered open the door and strode to the sanctuary of his room, silently daring the rest of them to follow. That could very well be the final straw to make him snap.

Caz spent the remainder of the day preparing for the night to come. Centering himself had never been more important. Meditation and yoga helped him find that inner pool of calm. A long, hot soak in the bathtub, followed by an equally long shower added weight to his ritual.

He met Nick downstairs shortly before they were scheduled to depart. The scent of his mother's roast beef hit him hard, reminding Caz he hadn't eaten since breakfast. Hunger rumbled his stomach, undoing all the good he'd spent hours perfecting. Nick arched his eyebrow at the sound, but said nothing. He'd dressed as Caz had, as they always did—long-sleeve black shirt and matching trousers, black leather shoes. The soft material and flexible shoes allowed for ease in movement, better control in situations where safety was paramount. None of the men in their circle of the community did full-on leather. With mastery came responsibility, and they all took that very seriously.

The closer Nick's sporty black Charger took them to Marvin's Malibu home, the more the mantle of Dominant settled on Caz's shoulders. He could feel the shift in his brother, too. Every so often Caz caught Nick's smile as he wove through traffic and lost any paparazzi tailing them. Power at its finest. Although if anyone managed to track them, all they'd learn was that he and Nick went to their lawyer's house for a social event. They could draw their own conclusions from that point on; they did that anyway.

Golden light glowed from low lanterns edging the Keating driveway and beamed from recesses in the arches guarding the deep-set porch of the white stucco two-story. Citrus trees protected the home from direct view, low shrubs, a concrete wall, and wrought-iron gates took care of the rest.

The parking apron off to one side of the driveway was half-full. It was hard to judge whether he and Nick had arrived early or late since no one knew how many were invited to this particular event. He did recognize most of the cars there—people who often attended, several of whom he'd done scenes with in the past. It was the other vehicles, those he didn't recognize, that intrigued Caz. One of them had brought tonight's mystery woman, someone he guessed was looking for at least a ménage, based on what Marvin had told him earlier.

Marvin opened one side of the double front doors when they approached. That had to mean someone was anxious to get started. Caz tried not to let the lady's impatience lead him. She wanted him and Nick for a reason—to cede total control to them. Her trying to top them at this point wasn't going to get any of them anywhere.

Marvin's smile was bright as he waved them inside. Caz heard the low tones of conversation in the adjacent main room. Heavy appetizers, tea sandwiches, and bite-size desserts would be waiting for guests to enjoy at their leisure, served by others within the community who lived to do so. Scenes were being planned over tasty food and cool drinks, to be executed privately or for an audience. No alcohol, no drugs—a variety of hot teas and cool fruit beverages only. Clear heads prevailed…always.

"Your timing is impeccable, gentlemen. As always." Marvin guided them toward his library—the opposite direction from the main gathering. "The other party has arrived and is waiting downstairs. She's asked me to go over the scene with you first."

"Is this her first time?" Nick asked as the door closed behind them.

"Her first ménage, toys notwithstanding. She's put a lot of thought into this and knows I wouldn't put her with anyone I didn't fully trust." He didn't invite them to sit, just thrust typewritten information into their hands.

Caz nodded as he read. Standard yellow light/red light safe words. No canes or blood drawn. Oral sex, yes. Anal sex…well, that was a given considering what she wanted. No blindfold. Bondage, yes, but no handcuffs. No humiliation.

He handed the paper back to Marvin. "No problems here."

"Agreed," Nick added.

Marvin smiled. "Good, then I'll take you to her." He dashed for the door. It seemed he had a lot of personal interest in this particular scene. Too much?

"Uhm…do you plan to watch?" Caz asked.

His step faltered. Eyes wide, he swung around. "No, I merely want to make sure all is well before I leave the three of you alone. She's placed tremendous trust in me. I don't want to give her cause to doubt that."

"Why would she?" Nick frowned. "You know we wouldn't—"

"Just come with me," he said. "Please."

Caz and Nick shrugged and followed him from the room. Quick steps led them to the to-die-for basement. It covered the full width and length and was divided into smaller sections. Unconfirmed rumor claimed it had once been a daycare facility back in the day. Caz had a feeling that story had been circulated for shock value, to add to the forbidden lure of the place. In any event, the private rooms made for perfect playrooms. Each had plenty of maneuvering space and every piece of furniture one would ever wish for, to do whatever one wished, in any way possible, with a full array of equipment with which to indulge. Walnut cabinets disguised king-size Murphy beds, easily lowered with the press of a button. There was also the added pleasure of a full-sized bathroom in the rear of every room to rival the plushest of resorts: thick towels, garden tubs, huge showers with nozzles in the most convenient places. Only the best and finest for Marvin's guests. It's why his invites were so sought after—comfort and safety, always safety.

Marvin's pace quickened. He led them to the middle room down the wide corridor, hand out for the door ten feet before they reached it. He hesitated when he wrapped his fingers around the knob, pulled in a breath and pushed it out in a *whoosh*, then twisted and opened. He stepped to one side to allow them in.

Caz's breath caught at the sight of long black hair drifting down the woman's slender back. She was draped in blue-black satin that shimmered from the light cast by dozens of candles filling the room, just like that gorgeous fall of wavy hair. She turned her head slightly to look at them over her shoulder. His gaze locked on the shift of her hair, the glimpse of her long neck, smooth angle of her jaw, and—

"Red light," Nick snapped. "Big, fat red light."

CHAPTER 3

Breathe.

It was impossible. Brooke was frozen in place, nipples thrust against the satin robe, mouth agape, eyes locked to Caz's. The moisture that had pooled in her crotch doubled with the intensity she saw in his deep brown gaze. Neither of them blinked.

Nick's voice rose in the background—white noise to her foggy head. Brooke tried to focus on what he was saying—*red light.* He didn't want to do this. Brooke could surely relate to that right now. But why the hell couldn't she speak up and add her own safe word? Better question...why didn't Caz? He merely stood there, staring at her...just like she stared at him.

From the corner of her vision she saw Nick slice his hand through the air. "There is no way in hell I'm doing this. This is bad form, Marvin, tricking us into this."

Marvin stabbed his finger in Nick's direction. "You don't want to do this? Fine. Don't." His arm swung their way. "But they aren't leaving until they resolve whatever's going on between them. I'm sick of the tension between them. It didn't matter before, but it damn sure matters now. We all have way too much to lose."

"Both of you calm down." Caz's voice was that of the peacemaker, soothing and inviting reason.

So different from what Brooke had experienced with him. She didn't know whether to relax or be on her guard.

"Brooke and I would like to be alone."

If she could have spoken, she might have disputed that. Or maybe not. One of the men grunted, then both left. As the door clicked shut, Caz slowly walked her way. His gaze never left hers. Her heart pounded with each step. She was conscious of swallowing when he lifted his hand toward her.

"Breathe, Brooke," he said, and brushed his knuckles over her cheek.

Her body behaved as if it had been waiting for his command. Blessed oxygen seeped into her system. She closed her eyes and drank in the feel of his hand against her face. Who knew his touch could feel so delicious?

"It appears as though we've found the common ground you mentioned earlier today." He dusted his fingers down her neck, then traced the skin along the edge of the robe collar. His thumb wandered up the column of her throat, circled over her chin, then came to rest on her lower lip.

"First time?"

"No." Somehow she'd managed to push the word out, not squeak it out. Still, she cleared her throat before continuing on. "A ménage, yes. Marvin's known for some time that I wanted to have a ménage. He assured me he would never place me with men he didn't trust one hundred percent. Clearly, he feels you and Nick are the ones." She added a small smile. "Despite his desire for us to 'resolve whatever is going on.'"

His hand drifted down her neck once more, wandering back to the robe's deep plunge. "He's done an excellent job of making sure our paths haven't crossed here before."

But that's what made Marvin's gatherings so perfect—he ensured all his guests were compatible. "He's done an even better job of bringing us together now," she said. "Would either of us have shown up if he told us who our partner was?"

"True enough. But now that the door is open..." He smiled and dropped his hand, only to slip her fingers into his. Fire raced up her arm and licked around her nipples before shooting to her crotch.

"How...how unfortunate Nick doesn't agree. I was looking forward to finally doing it." This time her voice did quiver. If he stood any closer her nipples could reach his chest. What would he do if she leaned forward and rubbed them over him? Of course, that would require she move, and Brooke was still frozen in place—Little Red Riding Hood cornered by the Big, Bad Wolf. And more turned on than the law allowed.

"The night's still young." Caz gave a subtle shrug. "Perhaps Nick can be persuaded to change his mind. If not"—another shrug of his shoulder—"well…we both need some relief. I'm sure we could find some together."

Her brain and body conflicted. Until five minutes ago, Brooke couldn't imagine a more unlikely partner, though, honestly, being near him did things to her she couldn't put into words. Now, standing here, his thumb making love to her hand, Brooke couldn't imagine anything better.

"I-I trust you," she stammered.

Caz lifted his eyebrows. "No, you don't. Oh, you want to, but you don't…yet. I'm not sure I trust myself. After all, aren't we both the reason the other is here? To release the tension of our meeting today? You need to release control. I need to pull it back in. Seems rather like Fate that we should be here now facing each other."

She tilted her head to one side. "But doesn't it say more that we're standing here *willing* to trust each other?"

"True," he said with a nod, then took a step back. "I suppose there's no better time to start than right now." He held out his palm. "Give me the belt from your robe, then lose the robe."

Brooke's heart jolted with the command. Adrenaline flooded her system. He was the Master; she must obey. Or they could both walk out that door and never look back. She knew she would always wonder what-if. Steady fingers loosened the belt, slipped it from the loops, and draped it across his palm. Without hesitation Brooke shrugged the satin robe from her shoulders and let it fall to her feet. Any other man would have ogled her nude body. Caz didn't. She appreciated the respect, still amazed from whom it came…and that she liked it so well.

"Hands behind your back." He moved behind her when she instantly complied.

He twined the satin belt around her wrists and secured them in a firm, yet not-too-tight knot. The ends fluttered down, tickling the crack in her ass.

"Beautiful." The word came out as awestruck wonder. Caz cupped her shoulders, nudged the curtain of hair to one side with his nose, then dropped a kiss to her shoulder.

Brooke closed her eyes on a sigh.

"Uh-uh"—he dropped his hold, denying her his touch—"eyes wide open."

"Yes—"

"Caz," he interrupted. "Not sir. Not Master. Caz. You might be the bottom, and I might be the top, but we are equals in this liaison."

"Yes, Caz." God, he was tripping up her heart and emotions.

"Sit on the table, heels locked around the legs, thighs wide." His hand touched the middle of her back, giving her a little push. More an encouragement than an order to obey.

Brooke assumed the requested position and watched as he walked to the ivory cabinet in the corner of the room. Candles flickered with the air he stirred. Goose bumps peppered her skin. Behind those high-polished doors lay every implement they would ever care to use and a few Brooke never wanted near her. Her eyes widened when he lifted the small single-tail whip from the array hooked on the inside of the door. Long fingers flexed around it. Her heart rate tripled when the tip dropped to the carpeted floor. It looked like a black snake against the sage green pile.

"I think it's a little too bright in here, don't you?"

It wasn't a question Brooke needed to answer. The scene had started, and she knew her place. Still, her eyes widened when Caz swung the whip. She jumped at the crack, then held her breath when he swung again.

Crack! The flame on his target candle went out.

Crack! Another extinguished immediately.

Crack! Crack! Crack! One by one the candles died. His aim was true—overhand, underhand, backhand, and forward.

The wet spot beneath her on the table grew.

Crack! Crack! Crack! Until only twelve candles remained of the dozens in the room. Then he turned his full focus her way, whip snaking behind him as he took one step, then two steps toward her.

"Lay back on the table. Heels perched at the corners. I want you open fully to me. I know it might not be comfortable on your arms, but don't worry…I'll be quick."

And merciful? Please add merciful. But she did as he'd told her, easing backward onto the edge, lifting her feet to the assigned position, letting her thighs fall wide open. Her breasts shook with every breath. She watch Caz's arm lift and squeezed her eyes shut in anticipation of the slice of leather.

"No, no," his voice sing-songed. "Eyes open."

She forced her lids open. Panic set in, threatening to hyperventilate her. One word would stop it all. One word. Then the whip cut the air. It landed with a resounding *snap* on the table between her thighs. Her pussy swelled in the resulting breeze.

Caz raised his arm again and followed with another lash. It struck the table above her shoulder. Another hit the other side. Again, between her legs. Brooke groaned with the impact as it hit the table. The lashes came quicker, just as they had with the candles. Brooke watched each one hit the targets around her, never once touching her skin. Crazy how her nipples and clit stood at attention, wanting a taste for themselves.

Caz stood beside her and dangled the tip over her aching nipples, then let it wander down to tease her clit. Brooke moaned and lifted her pelvis for more.

"I have never seen a more fuckable woman." His voice alone came close to bringing her to orgasm.

"Stand," he said. "Legs astride."

He cupped her upper arm to help her balance. He didn't know how close he was to having her writhe against him. Daring a glance at the swell in his trousers doubled her predicament. As if sensing her intent, Caz stepped away and let her find her position. Once she had, the whip kissed the carpet at her toes. Every crack rippled through her, making her want, need…crave.

Her mind adrift on a sea of pleasure—both real and imagined—she floated back to real-time when she realized Caz was standing beside her, nude. She longed to drink in the sight, but didn't dare break the spell. Too late she saw his arm swing. She sucked in a breath when she realized he'd aimed between her legs. A squeal died in her throat when he snapped his hand before her and caught the tip before it could reach her.

Brooke's pants for air cut off on a groan when he tucked the leather between the folds of her pussy. He tickled the tip over her nipples and sawed the leather over her clit.

"Don't come yet," he warned. "Wait for me."

Before she could wonder what he meant, Caz tucked against her and rested his hot cock in her bound hands. She looped her fingers around it and wiggled her ass into him. He rocked into her, flicking her clit under the whip. Pre-cum licked her back. She could feel the nerve in the under-ridge of his penis pulse with impending orgasm.

"It's going to be quick for me," she whispered.

"Me, too," he grunted, and stabbed his fingers into her.

Bodies locked into the first spasms of orgasm. Brooke crested and groaned with him as he spurted into her hands, onto her back. Her juices poured over his fingers. Suddenly her wrists were freed, but she used the freedom to caress his balls, milking more out of him. Caz's arm kept her anchored to him as he eased them to the floor.

"Now do you trust me?" His voice caressed her ear.

"Yes." *God, yes!* She cupped her cum-soaked hand over his.

Caz turned his hand and laced their fingers together. "Thank you. Thank you for this."

"Are we…done?"

"Not by a long-shot, sweetheart." He traced his tongue around her ear, then nipped the lobe. "I haven't eaten since breakfast. Let's take advantage of Marvin's hospitality and…other things."

"I'd like that," she said with a smile. "I'd like that a lot."

CHAPTER 4

It was hard to believe that the one woman responsible for undermining Caz's control was also the same woman who returned control to his hands. Peace seeped into his bones like nothing Caz had ever experienced, and he'd experienced a lot since he'd entered this community. Her unknowing gift humbled him beyond words, but somehow dropping to his knees before her in eternal thanks didn't seem wise. She'd trusted him when fear raced her heart—he'd seen the frantic flutter of her pulse at her throat. Nothing in the world would make him destroy that trust. She'd relinquished control to him, and Caz was going to see she never regretted it.

He inhaled the scent of her as he nuzzled her neck. A woman like this should be treated with respect. She stood there, spooned against his body like she belonged there. Her cum-soaked fingers laced with his.

"We should clean up first. Would you allow me the honor of doing that for you?"

"Of course." Her soft voice rolled over him like a benediction.

Smiling, she released his fingers and wiped her hands over her breasts. His semen glistened on her, begging to be licked off. Her nipples peaked and darkened, lifting in invitation. Tempting…oh-so-tempting. But she'd given control to him, and Caz wasn't about to let her down.

"Very clever yet subtle attempt at topping me." He flicked one nipple, then rubbed his palm over her butt cheek.

"Thank you." She beamed a smile over her shoulder, then squeaked when he pinched her backside.

"I'd threaten you with a little over the knee discipline..."

Her nipples hardened all the more with the catch in her breath. How wet would he find her now? It was almost too much to resist.

"...however, first things first."

He draped his arm around her and led her to the bathroom. Halfway there he indulged his need to thumb her nipple. Her groan quaked his knees and resurrected his flaccid penis. Caz let her know it, too, rubbing the length over her hip. Her gaze dropped, then she glanced up at him from under those long, dark lashes. He cupped her chin on the crook of his finger and lifted it ever-so slightly...then covered her mouth, plunging his tongue between her lips without hesitation.

She tasted like honey and lemon, her tongue soft as velvet and definitely not shy about dueling with his. In other words, she gave as good as she got without forcing the lead back to herself. Caz imagined her hovering over him, mouth working his cock while her tongue twirled around the head. He pulled her hip closer, nailing her body to his. His erection thanked him.

Brooke clutched his bicep and stretched on tiptoe, seeking more. Caz kneaded her lips until a mutual groan pulled them apart and left them panting. He tucked her under his arm and steered her onward.

Ceramic tile in shades of sand, coral, and sky cooled their feet. Caz wasted little time marveling over the beach-cottage décor. He snagged a thick washcloth from the heated towel bar and positioned Brooke before the triple mirror. Without question or instruction, Brooke braced her palms on the marble sink counter while Caz soaped the cloth under hot water. When he glanced up, it was to find her striking blue eyes locked on his reflection, measuring him from head to hip. The beauty of the room paled in comparison.

He took his time circling the cloth over the remnants of orgasm. She sighed with every stroke, lifting her body into his touch. He ached to be inside her, to fuck her until she screamed with climax a dozen times before he came. But he also loved the anticipation of the act, the control he mastered in waiting, despite the urge clenching his balls.

"You're well stretched here?" He dipped the cloth down her crack, reveling in her sharp intake of breath.

"Yes," she whispered, then cleared her throat. "I've wanted a ménage for as long as I can remember. I wanted to be prepared when the right moment came along."

"You'll have it tonight," he promised. "I swear it. I won't have you disappointed. You'll get what you need with me…what you want."

He tucked the cloth between her legs, caught the tip in front, and dragged it up through her labia. Brooke arched into her moan, eyes closed, lips parted.

"I'm going to spank you now."

Her eyes flashed open, fingers curled into the counter. God, he could smell her arousal thicken. "Assume a comfortable position, hands or elbows on the counter, feet back, your beautiful ass up. I'll be right back."

Caz forced himself to take his time going to the cabinet to retrieve an instrument of discipline. By instinct honed from years of practice, he realized Brooke's rush came from the threat and anticipation of pain, not pain itself. That was fine with him. Any fool could inflict pain, but it took a real master to dance that fine line without going over it.

His dick led the way, but Caz already knew the item he'd select—a leather paddle. A hard rub, a few well-placed pops… Caz smiled. It'd fire them both up in anticipation for the main event later. If Nick agreed. And Caz was damned determined to see he did. He had more than a few insights into his brother's turn-ons and knew exactly how to make a ménage with Brooke impossible for Nick to resist.

His hand fell to the leather paddle the second Caz opened the cabinet. The handle fit his hand nicely, giving him a good grip. He rubbed it against his stomach as he forced himself to maintain a measured stride back to Brooke. The leather was smooth, soft, and would be kind to her ass…if applied with the promise of force and not the force itself. It could also give a whack that would make a bottom think twice about sitting for a week. A versatile tool in the hands of one who knew how to use it.

His erection leaped at the sight of Brooke readied for him. She had elbows on the sink board, her hair a dark curtain around her face, nipples scuffing the marble surface. *Lucky marble.* Her back curved in a graceful arch to her upthrust bottom, feet shoulders' width apart. Moisture clung to her labia, daring him to have a taste. He tore his gaze away, but still found himself licking his lips when he glanced into the mirror and found those deep blue eyes watching his every move. She caught him without trying, and on some level they both knew that.

"I've always thought you were a beautiful woman"—he brushed the paddle over her butt cheeks—"but I never guessed how perfect you'd be. To think of all the time I've wasted—"

"All the time *we've* wasted," she softly added.

Caz conceded the point with a tilted nod and gave her a firm but gentle pop. Warmth rushed her body, adding a pink flush to her ivory skin. Another tap to the other side pulled her lower lip between her teeth. Another and pleasure dilated her pupils. He rained light pats on her ass until she writhed and moaned into every one. His cock felt close to splitting. Pre-cum dripping from the tip rivaled the juices sopping her crotch. Waiting for sex had never been more excruciating. If he didn't fuck her now, Caz knew he'd be all over her once they joined the group. He didn't want that for her. She wasn't a show or a prize to flaunt in front of others.

He traced the edge of the paddle up her spine, smiling with the subtle ripples under her skin. He set it aside and brushed his fingers back down her spine, into her crack, and right to her wet pussy. He thrust inside, cock surging when she clamped her muscles onto his fingers. He'd be lucky to last ten seconds inside her.

Caz tucked up behind her and rested his erection in the cleft of her body. Brooke clenched her cheeks, trying to pull him even closer. He said nothing, merely fumbled in the cabinet drawer for the condoms he knew were there. Her blue eyes approved every action. He couldn't look away.

"Your ass is nice and warm." One jerk ripped open the package.

"You should feel inside me." Her husky tone tightened his balls.

"I intend to." He rolled the condom into place, pivoted back, and plunged into her depths. "Damn!" he gasped.

He gripped her hips for fear her slightest movement would make him come. There wasn't anything he could do about the muscles caressing his dick. Caz closed his eyes against the fuck-me look in hers. The only sound in the room was his ragged breathing. An eternity ticked by before Caz thought he could handle it. Leaning over her, he slid his fingers around to her clit.

Moaning, Brooke arched into his touch, hips gyrating against him. All his efforts to hold back were for nothing. The surge in his groin put him right back on the edge. Caz clenched his teeth against orgasm, dared a slow stroke out…and then deep in. Sensation rolled over him. Fingers circled her clit, trying to find the right spot to send her to heaven, yet thwarted by her slickness. Each swipe tightened the hold Brooke had on him. Caz quit fighting. It was just too sweet.

He let their natural rhythm take over and gloried in how well-tuned to each other they really were. Her body sucked in every pounding thrust, drawing him in deeper, holding him tighter. Her clit swelled into his fingers, showing him exactly what she needed. And when she came, he knew what real heaven felt like. Her muscles squeezed his cock, demanding he join her. He couldn't remember when he'd been this hot, this hard, this desperate to come. He stabbed in hard and froze. His balls contracted, exploding jism along his shaft and out the narrow slit. Pain and pleasure had never felt so damn good.

One by one the white sparks beneath his eyelids faded. Brooke's hard breaths matched him in perfect time. He peeled her hair away from her neck and kissed her there. Her sigh squeezed his heart with the same intensity her pussy had his dick. Wrapping his arm around her waist, Caz brought them upright. Her reflection showed a woman well-sated yet ready for more—eyes bright, lips plump, cheeks flushed, nipples still hard as little rocks. Sharing her with Nick was going to kill him. But he'd give that to Brooke…because *she* wanted it. As for anyone else…not even if hell froze over.

Caz drew a line of kisses over her shoulder as he reached for the washcloth. "Now…where was I?"

With her dazzling smile, he cupped the cool cloth over her breast. Her gasp fired up his want all over again.

CHAPTER 5

Who knew she and Caz would be so perfectly matched? Obviously Marvin did because, after all, he'd arranged this little liaison.

Brooke marveled over her attire, handpicked by Caz minutes before. All he'd done was select a black brocade corset to wear over the satin robe, but she felt like a princess walking on his arm into the main room. No, better than a princess—like he treasured her. The glow in his face called her name. And his body—*God, his body!*—strong, determined, but never overwhelming her. He knew exactly what she wanted and needed and exactly how to give it to her. This from the man who'd glowered at her all this time. Brooke wasn't about to analyze the whys of it all. This was here and now, and she was going to enjoy every second of it.

"I see the perfect nest for us." Caz's whisper against her ear sent ripples over her skin, a cross between chill and the anticipation of a pleasure she'd only dreamed of finding until tonight.

Fingers laced through hers, he led the way. Black and red pillows ringed the sunken living room, the center of which was empty and waiting for whatever show others wanted to give. Marvin frequently changed the color scheme for his events as fit his mood or that of his guests. Tonight it screamed passion and sensuality, darkened harems and the forbidden, the promise of fulfillment and every fantasy come true…as long as one's focus remained on the arrangement of the body-sized pillows. The stage clashed horribly with the powder blue walls and ivory wainscoting. Ambient lighting and strategically placed candles helped draw attention from that.

Reid sat at the far end where he could watch the door for her—ever the protective big brother. They'd taken the journey into the community together, more or less, when they shared an apartment in college. No secrets with paper-thin walls. Reid had walked the path before her, sharing his experiences and knowledge gleaned. Brooke followed a year later, secure in the fact Reid was always nearby if she needed him.

She smiled and gave him their pre-arranged signal that all was well—a nod, followed by a subtle "okay" sign with her hand. Reid grinned and lifted a toast her way, then shifted his body toward the beach-tanned couple flanking him.

"Someone you know?" Caz asked.

"My brother."

"Small world," he said. "I've known him for a while, though I never knew his name or anything else about him."

Which was typical in this environment. Being here wasn't about networking.

"Do any scenes together?" she asked, though it really wasn't any of her business.

"Yes, when a third party was needed for whatever," Caz replied without hesitation, but didn't elaborate. He didn't need to. "You?"

"Yes, mostly at the beginning to ease my worries and his concerns that I get what I needed and wanted. Nothing…illegal."

"Nick and I like to have each other's back, too." A gentle push against her lower back urged her onward.

Caz selected a spot for them halfway down the circle, and directly across from Nick. Caz sank into the pillows and drew her with him, cradling her in the cove of his thighs. Warmth enveloped her, protecting her from the world. Her hero, handsome prince, knight in shining armor all rolled into one formidable package until tonight. She nestled against him, loving the feel of his body surrounding her, his hard cock her backrest.

The instant they settled, a server in flowing red satin appeared. Her cleavage spilled from her plunging neckline, revealing rouged nipples. Caz ignored the display. Sighing with contentment, Brooke draped her arms over the one he'd curled around her waist.

"Something to drink?" the woman asked.

"Cranberry juice and club soda. Two ice cubes, no more," he replied. "Have the boy bring a tray of assorted fruit, sandwiches, and chocolate."

"Yes, sir." The woman bowed lower, then straightened and sashayed away.

Brooke smiled. Caz's order was perfect. She hadn't had to think of a thing. It was the freedom she'd always wanted. In a world where she was forced to take the dominant role in business, Brooke had longed to leave that person at the door in her personal life. Finally, she had it.

Thank you, Marvin. She couldn't help wondering if Reid had a hand in this, too. He knew how important this was for her.

But could she keep this after tonight? *Two-way street. No analyzing allowed tonight. Enjoy the moment.*

In less time than it took to order, a male server in skin-tight black leather pants and vest delivered their tray of food. An erection swelled his fly, and Brooke couldn't help but notice the cock ring at the base ensuring it remained that way. He bent close, tray offered before him. The lust in his eyes was all for Caz.

Caz ignored him. "Leave it and go. Don't bother us again unless I send for you."

"Yes, sir," the man breathlessly replied.

No doubt Caz had made the man's night. Servers here lived to be ordered and dominated. Caz could tell the man to suck him off and the guy would do it. Or bare his ass for fucking, or bring the strap and bend over and…

The slice of a crop cutting the air jerked Brooke's attention to the right, where one male was getting just the taste of discipline he craved. His cheeks caved in with every suck of the cock before him. The recipient fisted the server's hair, forcing him to take it all, while another male laid stroke after stroke against his bare ass. Brooke felt every one in her clit and slowly slipped one leg over the other to relieve the ache.

After twenty-five strokes, he flung the crop aside, grabbed his sheathed cock and plunged into the server's ass. Whipper grabbed server's cock and squeezed as he pounded into him. Blow job clenched his jaw and thrust wildly into server's mouth. Muted groans filtered over the room.

Behind her, Caz's cock throbbed. It doubled Brooke's predicament. Her pussy swelled to agonizing proportions as she imagined him in the trio, taking charge and making sure everyone knew it.

She glanced up at him. He stared, unblinking, at the ménage. "Have you ever done that?"

His gaze clicked down to hers. "Man on man?" He looked back at the three. "No." Was that longing in his eyes? Then he smiled at her. "I'd be lying if I said I wouldn't want to try it at least once." He traced his fingers over her cheek. "And one of the many things I will never do is lie to you." He dropped his hand to her belly, resting between her navel and crotch. The heat spreading was sweet. "But, like you, I've never found that totally safe environment in which to do so. I talked to Nick about it, wondering if he could think of some way to do it that hadn't occurred to me. He agrees the idea is intriguing, but he's not interested in it for himself. He had no thoughts on whom to approach."

And at this stage of his career, Caz had to be very careful. Being in this particular community and engaging in the occasional ménage and Dom/sub game was one thing. Being linked in a male/male situation…there's was no telling how that would play out in this day and age.

Brooke's gaze wandered toward the frenzied fucking. Around the circle men and women masturbated themselves and each other. It was hard not to get caught up in the moment. Even Reid had one hand in the woman's pussy and the other wrapped around her partner's cock.

"Which role would you want to play?" she asked.

Cupping her breast, Caz circled his thumb around her hard nipple. "My answer might shock you."

"I'm braced," she said, squeezing her thighs against the ache building between them.

He chuckled. Brooke loved the sound, loved how it rumbled through her.

"Well…I trained thoroughly to be the dominant party," he said.

That would mean he'd spent some time being a bottom to learn how it felt. Odd the thrill that gave her.

"I've been in every one of those positions before, just not with a man…except for the whipping delivered by a male when I first began. It was memorable. He wanted me to get a real feel for the differences and what my responsibilities as a top would be. It was valuable lesson. Once I'd learned disciplinary techniques, I had to practice on him until he thought I was ready."

Fingers absently caressed the V of her crotch while his erection beat against her. "Anyway, I'm not saying a mouth is a mouth, or an ass is an ass. I know there are differences, both subtle and not so subtle. Having oral sex with a man or performing anal sex on one doesn't interest me in the least, but somehow the idea of being fucked by a cock and not a dildo…" His breath tickled her ear. "So…is it different?"

The barest hint of a nipple pinch shot sparks to her clit. "It's hotter," she gasped out. So much information they exchanged in so few words.

Three simultaneous groans sent more tremors through her—Caz, too, judging from the pulsing heat wedged against her back. Around them others came with the trio, and weren't shy about letting anyone know it. Before the gasps could die, the female server was standing before Caz and Brooke with their drinks. Her skin was flushed from the sex drama. Brooke could smell arousal on her. Or was that her own?

"Go," Caz ordered as he took the drinks. "If we're still here in thirty minutes, bring us the same."

She bowed and left without another word, eyes gleaming with pleasure. Brooke tried not to laugh. She wondered if this was what Caz had been doing to her all this time—trying to assert his dominance, and the only person who'd understood that was Marvin.

She wrapped her fingers around the cold glass when he handed the drink to her. A sip calmed the fire inside, but then he held a small sandwich to her lips so she could take a bite and fire raged once more at the intimacy. She bit it in half and he took the rest—cucumber with lemon pepper and the hint of cream cheese.

"My favorite," she said.

"Mine, too." He gave her another and took one for himself.

She snuggled into him and glanced across the room at Nick. He stared right back with that unblinking perusal that had to be genetic.

Two busty women—one blond, one brunette—flanked his brother, neither shy about making their wants known as they took turns stroking his thighs, erection, and balls. The fact he seemed to be ignoring them made them even more determined to get him to notice. The blonde raked his black shirt open and latched onto his nipples with teeth and blood-red nails. Not to be outdone, the brunette fished his penis from his trousers and went down on him. Nick look…bored. That only made them more aggressive.

"He seems unimpressed," she said as she accepted a taste of pineapple from Caz. Flavor burst over her tongue.

"Nick prefers a more subtle approach," he said. "Right now he considers them pesky flies. Any minute now he'll—"

Nick grabbed the brunette's neck and hauled her off his dick. Shooting her a glare meant to kill, he pushed her away and stuffed his manhood back where it belonged.

"I know my brother well." Caz spanned his hand against her midriff and brushed his thumb over the underside of her breast. "Uncross your legs, give him a flash of thigh, then ease the robe closed as if it's an afterthought."

His lips covered hers before Brooke could carry out his instructions. The kiss was slow and sweet, inviting her to ride the waves with him, showing her in that unique way she'd learned was all his that he treasured her. Emotion clogged her throat. She was conscious of doing as he'd ordered, but her body wanted more. Brooke rolled over, draping her hands up his hard chest, arms around his neck, straddling him until she could feel his cock tucked in the cleft of her body. She felt cool air against the backs of her thighs and just as quickly it was gone. He'd flashed her assets Nick's way.

Caz peeled his mouth from hers. "Now…toe those stilettos heels off…slowly. Give him a good look at your feet and ankles."

"Seriously?" She tried not to laugh.

Caz merely arched his eyebrow and dug his fingers into her butt cheeks.

Biting a gasp, Brooke dropped her gaze. "Sorry, Caz. I forgot my place. It won't happen again."

"Somehow I doubt that."

One hand anchored on her ass, he slipped the other in front. Slowly he peeled her robe open until her thighs were exposed. Her clit peeked up at him. He raked two fingers between her labia and clamped them over it. Brooke pressed her lips tight to keep her moan contained. It still managed to squeak out. She closed her eyes at the pleasure that rolled over her.

"Eyes open." He squeezed harder, doubling her predicament.

Brooke flashed her eyes open to his, mouth open, begging for his tongue.

"How did you manage to slip us out of the scene so easily? First, the question and answer session, and now questioning my orders?" Caz shook his head as he tsked. "I can see you're going to continue to be a challenge." He grinned. "I like that. Keeps me on my toes. However…" He shifted into his role more fully. "Your lapse is noted and will be dealt with later in a private forum. I can deliver a spanking you'll feel for a week and not think twice about it, if I decide that's what you need. Now…do as you were told."

He plucked her finger from her clit. It wept at the loss. His hands dove beneath the robe, clutching her ass. Brooke stretched out and, one by one, removed the heels. When she had done so, Caz rolled her beside him. The robe gaped for a few seconds before he took his time pulling it closed.

"Tell me," he said, lifting a grape to her lips, "how should I punish your lapse?"

Something in his tone told her it was a rhetorical question. She looped her tongue around the fruit, but he held on.

"That's it. Show Nick how well you can suck cock. So…five hard strokes of a crop?"

Heat flushed her body. She licked at the grape once more, twirling her tongue around like she had his dick as they'd dressed. His eyes glimmered with suppressed delight.

"Bound and spread for a taste of the strap before I suck your hard little clit to the edge of orgasm and leave it there?"

Brooke groaned and closed her mouth over the grape, taking his fingers with it.

"You're really asking for a trip over my knee, aren't you? You'll think twice about that when you can't sit comfortably for the next couple of days."

She clenched her thighs to relieve the ache rising.

"Uh-uh." He wedged his hand between them, rubbing her clit through the satin.

Brooke gouged her nails into the pillows and tried not to writhe into the touch. She was so close to coming. So close.

"All right, you made your point." Nick shoved his hand under Caz's as he stretched out on her other side.

One circle and orgasm rolled through her. She floated back to the world to find each of the men braced on his elbow and smiling down at her.

"You two seriously owe me for this favor," Nick said.

"I'm sure you'll get even soon enough," Caz shot back.

"You can bet on that." He reached over Brooke's body for the tray of food, making sure his erection nudged her hip. "Now feed me. I need my energy before you take advantage of me."

"Enjoy it while you can, little brother," Caz told him. "There won't be a second time."

"We'll see." He smirked and, with a wink to Brooke, stuffed the tiny sandwich in his mouth.

CHAPTER 6

Her hands should be shaking, but Brooke had never been calmer in her life. Once she realized this was really going to happen—her biggest fantasy was about to come true—all reservations faded. They'd bonded over snacks and cranberry cocktails, amid kisses and caresses that fired her up and promised her a night they'd all remember.

Caz and Nick stood at the same time, as if they'd planned it all along, and held their palms out to her. Brooke slipped her fingers into their grasp and stood. They hugged her between them, arms and erections ensuring she was locked in their embrace. Their cocks beat in time to her heart—one wedged against her lumbar, the other to her belly—teasers for what they'd feel like inside. Two dominant males…and they were all hers.

Guarded between them, Caz and Nick led her from the main room and toward the basement stairs. Fingers delved into her robe, right to her nipples the minute they cleared the first threshold. Each tweaked and tugged, elongating the turgid flesh until her areoles were hard beads.

"Think how it'll feel when my teeth are around it, and Caz latches on to your clit." Nick's voice rumbled against her ear.

Her blasted eyes closed with her sigh. Caz's sharp whack on her ass popped them open. Juices dampened her thighs.

"Looks like someone needs a little discipline reinforcement." Nick pinched her nipple and rolled it between thumb and forefinger.

Caz chuckled. "Care to tell her what you'd do if she were yours?"

Nick laughed lightly. "No far teasing a man with what he'll never have."

Brooke's step faltered. Caz tightened his hold and kept her upright. Her lips formed an apology. He placed his finger on them to keep the words at bay.

"Okay, honey? Safe word needed?"

She *was* his. Nothing felt more perfect.

"I'm good. Just…surprised."

He cocked his head to one side, and she saw in his deep brown eyes that he knew what she meant.

"Me, too," he said with a smile.

Nick groaned. "You guys are killing me. Yellow light, please. This is way beyond having a scene. This is—"

Caz cupped his shoulder. "Brooke and I know what this is. The beginning of forever. Neither of us will deny that or even try to. We know how important this is. But I also know Brooke wants and needs this. I'd be hurting her not to see she has it. Just because we are moving into couple-dom doesn't mean she has to give up something she's wanted for so long. I won't have her wondering what-if. You'd do it for your woman. Help me do it for mine."

Being possessed had never felt so damn good. Brooke watched Nick's internal struggle in his eyes—fear of interfering warring with his desire to help fulfill this fantasy and do as his brother asked. And in those seconds she knew what she had to do.

"I think I know what might help," she told them. "Please, not another word. I'll be right back."

Brooke waited for their nod, then strode toward the main room. It was time to even the playing field, so to speak. If all parties agreed, it should ease Nick's mind. It would also fulfill not only her fantasy but Caz's as well.

Reid's gaze lit on her the second she appeared in the doorway. A flick of her finger motioned him her way. He was on his feet before another second passed, ignoring the couple who'd hung on his every word and touch. The furrow between his dark eyebrows deepened with every step he took. Brooke tried not to laugh. His devotion…other sisters should be so lucky. Few siblings would have experienced what the two of them had; Caz and Nick would be one of the exceptions.

"Something wrong?" He cupped her elbow and turned with her away from the room. He was calm, controlled, not ready to jump to conclusions.

"It's more than great, actually." She glanced up. "Hard to believe I'm saying this, Reid, but he's *the* one."

He chuckled. Tension faded from his muscles. "Ah…I see."

"I want this night to fulfill all our fantasies." She touched his arm, pulling them to a stop. "I want to give him you, too."

His gaze scanned her face and in those blue eyes, so much like her own, Brooke saw the same hesitation she'd seen in Nick's.

"Are we talking a ménage?" he finally asked. "You, him, and me?"

"A *ménage a quatre.*" And she managed to say it without blinking.

"Tricky maneuver for a first-timer."

"I understand I'm to be in the best of hands tonight."

Reid grinned. "And so you are." He jerked his head. "And your other partners are in agreement?"

"Let's find out."

Eyebrows arched—more curious than shocked—when Caz and Nick saw her return with Reid. Brooke kept her focus on Caz and walked up to him until her breasts pressed into his solid torso. She put her hand over his heart, feeling the rapid thud resonate inside her. Caz brushed his fingers over her cheek, then stabbed them into her hair. His erection kept time with her heartbeat, and Brooke knew she'd made the right decision.

"You're giving me your brother. I want to give you mine. Trust." A single word she knew he'd understand.

"It goes both ways." Caz nodded. "God, Brooke," he gasped, then kissed her forehead and clutched her head to his chest. She closed her eyes and drank him in.

Warmth surrounded them and she opened her eyes to see Reid and Nick at their sides, touching without touching.

"Let's get our rules and boundaries established." Nick combed his fingers through her hair.

A damn fine idea. Safety first, especially since they were going to be piled up or beside each other. And the sibling thing was going to be extra tricky. But they'd all been around the block with this stuff more than a time or two. All done scenes together in some form on the other, all seen each other's respective sibling have sex before, seen them naked. They all knew what to respect and understood that in situations like the one they were about to enter there was no way to avoid legs tangling. They were all very comfortable in their own skins or else they wouldn't be here.

"Absolutely." Caz swung her toward the basement stairs.

Reid and Nick let Caz lead the way, neither usurping his alpha role. His hand against her back comforted, protected, and made her hot as hell to feel it roam her bare skin, delve deep inside. Caz would take care of everything...*everything*.

He opened the door to their designated room, lifted her in his arms, and carried her over the threshold. The symbolism wasn't lost on her. This was the beginning of their future. He cradled her against him as he walked across the room. In their absence someone had relit the candles and lowered the Murphy bed. Plump pillows lined the headboard under niches that held condoms, lubricant, and various other toys. Crisp white sheets of the finest Egyptian cotton were turned down, inviting them in.

Caz placed her in the center of the bed and slipped her heels from her feet. They fell to the carpeted floor with a soft *thunk*.

"Undress and crawl under the sheet. You may play with your nipples discreetly, but not anything else." He brushed his fingers over her soles and up her calves. Pleasure rolled over her skin, lifting goose bumps. "I will be watching."

"Yes, Caz." Her portion of the scene had begun.

He helped her unhook the corset, peeling her robe back far enough to suckle her breasts to hard, aching points, then eased his fingers into her moist pussy, thumbed her clit, and left her wanting as he joined Reid and Nick to discuss the finer points of their ménage.

The men sank into the depths of the sofa facing her. Brooke kept her gaze on Caz as she let the robe fall from her shoulders. It was impossible to look at anyone else when his presence filled her so much. Muted conversation filtered her way. She heard none of it above the heartbeat hammering in her ears. In her fantasy-filled head, Brooke told herself they were deciding her fate.

From the corner of her eye, she watched the robe slither toward the floor when she lifted the sheet and slid beneath it. The line-dried scent wrapped around her. The cotton was soft and cool against her hot skin and hardened her nipples all the more. They craved to be touched, sucked to ripeness until they threatened to burst, until she felt the tug deep in her clit. She cupped her breasts, knowing her touch would never be enough to appease them, yet needing something, anything to help nurture the lust.

Brooke jumped and jerked her hands away when Nick snapped to his feet. She watched him walk to the cabinet, retrieve a flogger, and stalk her way, tails dragging at his side. So like Caz... *But not Caz.*

Eyes wide, she clutched the sheet to her chin like a virginal bride.

She jumped again when she felt a hand curl around her ankle.

"Trust, sweetheart," Caz said.

"I do."

"Good." He spread her legs wide beneath the sheet, then crawled between them and peeled her fists open. "You'll love it. I promise." He placed her arms beside her, licked over her collarbone, dove his tongue into the well of her throat…and left her aching once more.

Her gaze followed him back to Reid, then shifted to Nick as he replaced Caz at the foot of the bed. He dangled the tips of the flogger over her toes, then danced it up one leg and down the other, then up to the apex of her thighs where he gently dropped it. The handle rested between her breasts, heavy as a dick. The ends draped her pussy, kissed her clit. Brooke's juices soaked through the sheet and she swore her labia tried to grab the leather strands. Heat banked in her crotch, swelling everything to that bursting point she'd dreamt of only minutes ago.

Nick walked slowly to the right side of the bed, stripping as he went. Brooke tried to look his way, wanted to, but Caz's eyes held hers captive again. He and Reid were still talking, but his attention was hers…until Nick wrapped his hand around the flogger handle and eased the tails up her body. Breaths heaved her chest as he neared her breasts. He lifted the flogger until it barely touched her through the sheet, then he slapped it gently over her hard nipples.

Brooke groaned and fisted the mattress.

"Eyes open," Caz called out. "Or I might decide you don't deserve this tonight. Do you want to be forced to watch others do what you crave to experience?"

"No, Caz," she gasped out.

"I assure you, I don't like having to punish you, but I would be severely remiss if I neglected so basic a thing if you need it. Do you need it, Brooke? Shall I send the others away and spend the rest of the night reminding you over my knee? Or perhaps you need to have them witness your punishment? Maybe I should take you back to the main room and bend you over for strapping? Bind you with silken ties to the bench and let everyone watch your pussy weep as your ass gets hotter and hotter, redder and redder? Let you have the taste of a dildo, but nothing more. A hint of what you could have had if only…"

Her brain shut down. The thought…the image. She loved how he instinctively knew the words that would set her blood churning. *Oh, God!*

The whip cracked beside her hip. "Eyes…open."

"Yes, Caz." If he'd landed that snap between her thighs, she knew she would have come. "It's just so hard when it feels so good."

"I know, baby." He tickled the leather over her clit. "I know. It won't be much longer and you'll have the relief you need. We all will."

He barely stepped away before Nick started that sweet torture once more. Brooke thrilled in the smell of the leather as he danced it over her breasts, against her throat and cheeks, down to her pussy where he lingered until she thought she'd scream from the teasing. Just when she thought she'd found his pattern, Nick stopped and tossed the flogger aside.

The mattress dipped with his weight. She shifted her gaze to his naked body for the first time, admiring the similarities to Caz in the cut of his muscles, wondering at the differences in his cock, how it would feel pumping into her ass, how both of them would feel. He knelt beside her and reached for the condoms in the headboard. She licked her lips, tempted to taste the drop of pre-cum collected in the tip of his penis. Would it taste the same? How could she possibly resist? She inhaled his musky scent, then flashed her tongue over the crown.

Nick smacked his palms against the headboard and groaned. "God*damn*, she has a wicked tongue," he gasped out.

Caz chuckled. "Tell me about it. Sweetest thing this side of heaven." He jerked the sheet away from the bottom of the bed and crawled in between her legs.

Brooke expected a slow exploration up her thighs. Instead Caz went right to the source, sucking her clit hard between his lips. He swirled his tongue around and around, knowing exactly what she needed…and just when to stop.

She beat her fists into the mattress at the loss of orgasm. Caz merely grinned and straddled her chest while he grabbed a condom and Nick stretched out beside her. Grabbing his cock, Caz rubbed the tip over her lips. Brooke lapped up his pre-cum, hesitated…then sucked the crown in and gobbled him down until his tight balls kissed her chin. Caz's groan felt like victory. Glancing up at him through her lashes, she threatened him with her teeth, then licked him from root to tip and eased back into her pillow.

"Yep," he said, "very wicked." He sheathed his dick and slid next to her.

Strong arms wrapped around her, pulling her on top of his hard body while his mouth claimed hers. Brooke didn't hesitate. One plunge seated him deep. They froze, fighting the urge to go crazy, to make this last for all of them. She wanted to claw at his chest, ride him hard and fast, feel him fuck her so deep his cock kissed her tonsils.

His slow, even breaths calmed and centered her. She mirrored his breathing, letting it ease the fucking frenzy that wanted to erupt in her. He spanned his fingers against her back, massaging in slow circles as his lips kneaded hers, fucking her with his mind. Brooke tried to relax, but couldn't. She was all too aware of Nick reaching for something else, of him settling closer to her, of his fingers tracing down her spine and down and down. *Slow. Too slow.*

She gasped when his hand touched her anus. This was it—the moment she'd always wanted. It seemed anti-climatic when compared to the bigger gift she'd received tonight. Her body clenched with the first touch of lube against her ass. Two long fingers probed her, stretching her for what was to come. She wanted it more than she could bear. Her body clenched around Caz's cock. His muffled moan rumbled through her, absorbed in the kiss. His erection grew harder and hotter, making everything down there ache twice as much. Again he slowed his breathing, silently bringing her with him. Once she'd reached that quieter place with him, Caz shifted his legs, giving Nick more room to kneel behind her.

Nick jerked the sheet off the rest of the way. Cool air drifted over her back. Caz dusted the chill bumps from her skin, dotted kisses over her face, traced his thumbs over the sides of her breasts, then rested her head on his shoulder when Nick finally moved in.

Brooke whimpered at the sweet feel of his cock piercing the muscle. No matter how many times she'd toyed with cock and dildo, nothing compared to this. It was the heat from both dicks, she decided, the pulse throbbing through them, sending ripples of pleasure deep into her. Nick eased in, each inch he gained drawing heavier pants from him, from all three of them. This time there was no controlling it. When he reached the hilt, his body covered theirs. Holding her securely between them, Caz and Nick rolled until Nick was in the bottom position.

Weight dipped the bed once more.

Caz braced his strong forearms against the bed, trying to keep the bulk of the weight off Brooke and Nick. His eyes seemed to fall into hers, and she realized it was their souls bonding a little more. She kept her gaze on him, not on Reid moving in behind him. No one dared move. If they started rocking together now, none of them would last a second.

Caz swallowed against the push of Reid's fingers. Brooke could feel the stroke echoed in her body, in the beat of Caz's cock, the twitch in his sac. Reid pulled in a deep breath. Legs tangled with legs in an effort to accommodate everyone's comfort. Caz gasped. His forearms shook. Eyes rolled back in his head as his lids closed.

"God, baby," he whispered, "you were right. Much hotter."

Someone else groaned. Brooke didn't know who. Hell, it could have been her. She was so far gone with pleasure she couldn't think straight, but she could damn well feel. She let her mind and body drift. She didn't have to take charge or control anything. Someone else had the reins and it had never felt better and more right in her life.

The first thrust of body into body took her breath away. Caz followed with a deep plunge that Nick quickly echoed. She wrapped her arms around Caz's torso, wishing she could lock her legs around him, too. Another harder thrust went through them. Then another and another as the rhythm took hold. The glide was sweetly choreographed, like they'd done this a thousand times. She couldn't help it—she closed her eyes.

"Fuck!" Caz shouted. "I can't hold on. I never thought…"

Reid pushed deep, rolling into his climax, and grunted as he came. Caz's jaw clenched and Brooke could feel the battle in the throb of his dick as he fought off the inevitable. Nick's fingers dug into her hips. Brooke gripped Caz's back to keep from shoving Nick's hand to her pussy. Nick pumped into her ass and writhed into his orgasm. She and Caz lay there between the men, absorbing the spasms. She was so close, so close. The right thrust this way or that and…

Without warning she found herself on top of Caz. Before she could process how quickly they'd moved, she was under him once more, and Nick and Reid were panting for breath on either side of them.

Caz smirked down at her. "You closed your eyes."

"So did you," she said in return.

Caz licked his thumb and wedged it between them. The instant it touched her clit, he moved. Hard, pounding thrusts took her breath away. She locked arms and legs around him, never wanting it to end, never wanting to let go. The whip cracked the air, the flogger brushed her leg, her thigh. Another snap. Another brush. So much sensation. So many thrills wiggled through her, urging Brook to let go.

Caz rolled to his back, taking her with him. The flogger slapped her ass…and orgasm exploded from her. Caz growled with his release, grinding into her so deep she swore she truly did feel it in her throat. Brooke collapsed on top of him.

Cradling her in his arms, Caz rolled her beneath him. He kissed her everywhere he could reach without pulling them apart. After-love had never felt sweeter.

She didn't realize Reid and Nick had left until she heard the door click shut. God, how long had she and Caz lain here lost in ecstasy? Obviously, long enough for the other men to recoup and dress.

Smiling, she stretched around Caz, loving how great he felt in and on her. "The only thing that would make this any better would be if we could curl up and go to sleep." Brooke ran her fingers through the hair dusting his nape.

"I'd like that," he said with a grin. "Think you could make room for my toothbrush at your place?"

Brooke wrapped a hug around him. "I think I could make room for much more than that."

EPILOGUE

Well, ladies, another one bites the dust!

Holy cow! No one, and we mean no one, saw this one coming. The last we heard was that there was no love lost between Casper Tristan and Brooke Hansen. And that he staunchly opposed hiring her as Mesquite's manager.

But check out the photos for yourself. Some serious PDAs between hard-hitting Mesquite drummer Caz and beautiful, hard-charging, up-and-coming manager to the rock stars Brooke. Forget the rumors. The previously at-war couple have made no secret about the fact that Caz has already moved into Brooke's home. But this A-list twosome continue to play coy over marriage talk. In Caz's own words, "Why don't we keep you guessing?" When cornered away from her new love, Brooke is just as elusive saying, "I'm sure there will be a press release when that happens."

So does when mean it will? Come on, guys, throw us a bone. What happened? When? And how? Is that what's behind the sudden trip to Diversions in Palm Springs? Or is something else going on there, too? Talk is legendary rocker, Reno, is courting Brooke's managerial skills. Who knows, could she be luring Reno's former group Three back to perform? I know I'd be first in line to buy a ticket to see Mesquite and Three on the same stage again. They say magic happens at Diversions Spa and Resort, but that would take a miracle. But then no more so than Caz and Brooke hooking up.

It's been one revelation after the other with Mesquite. Brian married with children. Pablo and Ceci and the baby bump watch, no date yet for that wedding. And now steely-eyed Caz caught. With only one brother left to take the plunge, odds makers are wondering how long it will take before Nick succumbs. When that happens, hearts will break all over the world...mine included.

MAGIC MAN

CHAPTER 1

Gaby Keating stared at the lights all ablaze at her father's mansion. She should have called first. Under normal circumstances she would have, but this was critical. She couldn't give her father a chance to say no. He had to understand how very important this was. Another woman was dead, and their only suspect was a man who frequented closed circles. Places her father knew well. He was her entry into that community. It was the only way to catch a killer. But no one was more nervous than Gaby.

She laughed without humor. They were all nervous, and her father would be even more so. The assignment she'd proposed was beyond dangerous. She might be familiar with the BDSM community; her father was a major player. Her mother as well. But these were secrets the two always held close to their chests. They'd answered her questions those times she asked, even allowed her to watch from a distance when they were not directly involved in a scene, but there was never an invite to join. That request had to come directly from Gaby, at which point she would most likely be guided to a different circle that did not mesh with theirs. Until this moment, Gaby never dreamed she be considering it. But lives were at stake, their choices few.

Now she'd run smack-dab into one of her father's parties. The killer she sought could very well be inside, stalking his next prey, camouflaged under the guise of safety with a hidden agenda all his own. Gaby couldn't very well go through the front door. No one attended Marvin Keating's parties uninvited, and it was fairly clear from her jeans, boots, and navy T-shirt that she wasn't a part of their crowd. Her father would be alarmed at her unannounced arrival, the calm sophistication he needed to carry out his role tonight shaken. Back door was best.

She eased her car down the driveway and took the side road to the rear of the grand old house. Sodom and Gomorrah, her grandmother called it. She'd blamed the house and its owner a thousand times over for her daughter's "downfall." Cursed every day Gaby's mother was associated with Marvin Keating. Seethed that the man took his obligations as Gaby's father very seriously. She'd wanted something to hold against him, someone to blame for what she called the ruination of her only child. Their lifestyle was all she could target and she attacked it viciously. Gaby had resented her attitude more than her parents did, who merely shrugged it off. Once Gaby joined the police force and found *her* career choice under attack, she finally understood. Shrugging off the resentment was the only option. The old woman would have a coronary if she discovered her two greatest evils were about to merge.

If only. Gaby snickered, then scolded herself for the harsh thought.

She parked beside her father's Lexus on the garage apron. The man never parked inside the garage, said he didn't like the closed in feeling even with the door open. Claustrophobia was his Achilles' heel. Gaby wasn't too fond of it either.

She unclipped her badge and removed her shoulder holster, securing both in the locked console between the bucket seats. All she took was the folder with the crime scene photos—her ammunition to help convince her father to help her.

So far she hadn't been detected. This area was darker, the perfect spot for a rendezvous, but it looked like the main action was still centered within the house. Boot steps marked her stride toward the kitchen entrance, keys to the Keating kingdom clutched in her hand. Red brick, forest green tile, stainless steel, and cast iron glowed ahead. Barely dressed servers sauntered in and out in a constant stream, trays perched high, while the cook served up one treat after the other.

Gaby's stomach rumbled. Nobody's cooking could hold a candle to George Preston's. The man could make Cheerios a gourmet treat.

As if he sensed her thoughts on him, George glanced up from his work. His dark eyes lit with recognition. The hint of a smile curved his mouth. And just like that he masked the emotion and glared at the servers hovered about.

Gaby grinned. She couldn't hear the words, but judging from

George's scowl and the way he shooed his hands at the people, it was clear he wanted them gone, and now. She blessed him for giving her the chance to sneak in undetected. The instant the kitchen door swung closed, he was at the back entrance, opening it, his arms wide.

"Gabrielle, what a joy!" He wrapped her in a suffocating bear hug Gaby loved. "It's been forever."

She laughed and let him rock and squeeze her. "A month at best."

"Two. And I am counting." He held her at arm's length. His bald head reflected the light overhead. "But not the best of times for a visit."

"So I see." She patted his arms and gave him a kiss on the cheek. "But it was unavoidable. I have a work situation I need Dad's help with."

"Someone after you? Someone hurt you?" He wrapped his fingers around the handle of his most lethal butcher knife. "I'll cut his heart out."

She laughed again and touched his fingers. "Which might explain why I have so few dates."

"Hmph. You have so few dates because you're too wrapped up in your work." He shook his head with his tsk. "Just like your parents."

"You've got no room to talk." She tapped his bulbous nose. "It's a police matter I need Dad's help with. A private issue I wanted to discuss in person, not on the phone. Urgent."

"You go up." He steered her toward the back staircase. "I'll tell your father you're here."

"Thanks."

"Wait."

She'd barely gotten one foot on the stairs.

Glancing over her shoulder, she watched George pile a tray with sandwiches, fruit, and treats, especially treats. Chocolate confections that made Gaby's mouth water. How did George always know exactly what she needed?

"You eat." He shoved the tray into her hands, then tucked two bottles of spring water into a canvas bag and handed it to her. "Go."

"Thanks, George. I'm starving."

She propped the tray on her palm, her evidence folder flat beneath it, and tossed a piece of homemade fudge into her mouth as she trotted up the stairs before George could spew out his normal litany: *skin and bones, need more curves, work too hard.* His unique way of saying I love you. He'd been a fixture in her life for as long as Gaby could remember.

By the time she reached her father's suite of rooms, Gaby had polished off at least a half-pound of fudge and was well on her way to finishing the remainder. Sheer will forced her to considered one of the finger sandwiches. She eyed the two-bite morsel as she shouldered the door open.

Cucumber…yuck.

A chocolate-covered cherry made the cut instead. She bit into the shell and twined her tongue around the goo and cherry inside. Bliss…complete and utter bliss. About the only thing that would top it was a glass of merlot to wash it down.

Gaby sat the tray on the oak end table and sank into the long sofa. The cushions cradled her in comfort, inviting her to kick her boots off and rest. She'd always loved her father's rooms—deep clarets with cream colors woven throughout. It was quieter here than the rest of the house, cooler. *Sanctuary.* A comfort she'd never been able to reproduce in her own meager decorating efforts.

She eyed the glimmering bar in the corner of the room. The bottle of merlot called her name. Again she fought the urge down. Gaby wanted to be clear-headed when she talked to her father. She placed the folder on the coffee table, a match to the end table. He'd be furious over the pictures, not at her but at the beast who'd done such a thing. He might even want to take care of the matter in-house. Gaby hoped to appeal to his belief in the justice system. Fear for his daughter's welfare and the monster loose in his private community could very well tip those scales when weighed against his years as a powerful attorney.

Gaby left the folder closed and uncapped a bottle of water. She'd seen the pictures so many times she had every horrid detail memorized. Maybe her father had already heard rumors and rumblings and they could close the case now rather than risk her going undercover. Gaby knew she was hoping for the impossible. If Marvin Keating knew of such a thing, the doer would be behind bars.

She slugged down the water and eased into the cushions. God, she was tired. Scared, too. The thought of ending up like these women…

The door swung open. The alarm on her father's face yanked her guilt front and center. Worry deepened the subtle lines in his handsome face, paled his tanned complexion and made his white hair stand out.

He shoved the door shut behind him and hurried her way, arms outstretched. "Gaby…sweetheart…what's—"

"I'm okay, Dad. Nothing's wrong." She met him halfway, hugging him tight. "I need your help on a case. I don't know where else to turn."

Tension eased from his muscles. He let out a breath and led her back to the sofa. "Of course. Are you here officially or unofficially?"

"Officially...sort of." They sat side by side. "I told my people I had someone who might be willing to help, but I didn't divulge who that person was." She picked up the folder and handed it to him. "Warning...the photos are gruesome."

He'd seen a lot in his profession over the years, but Gaby still wanted to warn him. His barely perceptible flinch when he saw the pictures made her glad she had.

"Fire play gone bad," she told him.

"Are you sure?" His tone begged her to tell him she wasn't.

Gaby dropped her hand to his knee. "Both women have ties to that lifestyle. Both frequented the exclusive clubs. The suspect is six feet tall, bald, muscular, wears a lot of leather, and doesn't seem to have any body hair as far as we can tell."

His nostrils flared with his intake of breath. "Then lock him up." He flicked the folder closed and tossed it back to the table.

"Unfortunately, we lack a name, fingerprints, forensic evidence. He doesn't seem to be a regular, yet manages to hookup."

"Maybe he's snatching the victims from outside the clubs."

"In both instances it appears as though the women left willingly with him from inside the clubs. No surveillance. Both women had a reputation as no-holds-barred subs."

That widened his eyes. "Then they were as crazy and stupid as he is."

"And now very dead. Burn patterns show he took his time, too."

He scuffed his hands down his face. "You want me to put feelers out? I can do that."

Gaby rubbed her hand over his back. "I hate showing up here out of the blue, Dad, especially when you're entertaining. But we think we know where he might hit next."

"Good. You can stake out the place and nab him when he leaves. I'll make sure others are watching to see he doesn't slip the noose."

She braced herself for the imminent explosion. "That's not exactly what we need right now. We want to make sure the evidence is solid. We want to catch him in the act...more or less."

"Good God, Gaby! Endangering another woman—"

"Not just any woman. An undercover cop. Me."

He vaulted to his feet. "Have you lost your mind?"

Gaby flipped the folder open and spread the photos over the table.

Women violated and burned to death after slow, methodical torture. "Someone you know could be next."

"And it damn sure isn't going to be my daughter!"

Gaby matched his steely blue-eyed gaze with one of her own. *This* DNA clearly had passed her way—his determination and resolve. She'd learned from the master.

"God, Gaby…you're going to do it whether I help you or not, aren't you?"

A single nod replied for her. "Now…do I go in there safe, with all the skills I need to pass muster, or go in at risk?"

"Young lady…" He snapped a scolding finger in her face. "That's a damn dirty tactic. If you think for one minute… If your mother…" He dropped his hand and squared his shoulders. The stance shot her back to her teenage years. Dread slithered down her spine.

"Fine," he replied calmly. "You'll do what I say, when I say, with the people I designate. Understood?"

"Yes, sir." The ease with which she'd won spawned suspicion.

"Wait here," he said. "I'll be right back." He strode toward the door. "And you might want to swish the chocolate off your breath in the meantime."

Gaby waited until he shut the door, then stuffed another chocolate-covered cherry in her mouth. A small act of childish defiance, but it felt good.

CHAPTER 2

"I have to admit I'm pretty much spent."

Nick Tristan agreed. He and Reid Hansen had just engaged in the most intense foursome either of them had ever experienced. And they had experienced a lot. This was different. This involved their siblings, now cuddled under the covers in the room behind them. This involved the beginning of love. No one had seen that coming, yet no one could deny it, especially the new couple.

Nick smiled. It felt right, perfect, and tugged at his heart.

"I could use a drink." Nick finished buttoning his black silk shirt, then stuffed the tails in his black trousers. "And a shower."

Reid finger-combed his dark brown hair, then smoothed his blue shirt, a dark shade that matched his eyes. "I hear you on both counts. The shower might be doable here, but you know Marvin won't crack open the liquor cabinet for anyone during one of his events."

True enough. Marvin was a stickler for rules and protocol at his gatherings. High on the list was no alcohol served. Anyone who broke that rule left—immediately—never to return again under any circumstances.

"I doubt we'd be breaking any etiquette protocol if we left." Nick jerked his head toward the room they'd just left. "Caz can catch a ride with Brooke, so I don't feel bad about taking the car."

"She wouldn't leave him stranded." Reid flashed a megawatt smile. "Well, she might have before tonight, but now I'm pretty sure those two will be joined at the hip."

Nick grinned. "And other places, too." He clapped Reid on the shoulder. "My place or yours? Gotta warn you, my place is overly crowded with family at the moment."

"Then my place it is." They fell in step as they walked toward the stairs leading up from the converted basement playrooms. "I have a spare room. You can stay the night."

"Sounds like a plan." He and Reid had always gotten along well. Nick liked his company, which was a good thing since they were pretty close to being family now that Caz and Brooke had hooked up.

"I hope Marvin won't take offense over our leaving so early," Reid said as they trotted upstairs.

Nick laughed. "He's been dangling so many strings and has so many irons in the fire tonight he'll probably be glad of two less people to worry about." Nick motioned to the room they'd just left once more. "You realize he's responsible for that."

"I suspected. For a man who likes to make matches, he's a pro at avoiding one for himself."

"Ah, well." Nick shrugged. "When the time's right…"

"It'd take a clever, determined individual to catch our silver fox," Reid said.

"Might be a fun chase to watch."

"I agree. You bring the popcorn."

Laughing, they topped the stairs and ran right into the object of their discussion. Stern lines tightened Marvin's mouth. Nick's heart stuttered in fear Marvin had overheard and taken offense. Reid had gone stock-still beside Nick.

"Marvin…we were just look—"

"I need you both. Now. Come with me." Marvin pivoted and strode away, leaving them little choice but to follow.

Nick expected they'd be escorted back to the main event, or another private playroom, or even tossed out on their ears. Nothing surprised him more than when Marvin turned up the staircase to the private rooms upstairs.

He exchanged a confused glance with Reid as they followed. Deep pile carpet absorbed the sound of their footsteps. The colors at the top matched the powder blue and ivory wainscoting below, but the quiet, the loss of echo against the walls, faded to nothing. The first floor was the public showcase; the second was the heart of the home.

Marvin lengthened his stride, his target apparently a door at the far end of the hallway. It was all they could do to keep up. Nick's deep frown mirrored Reid's. Once they reached the destination, Marvin wrapped his hand around the handle and faced them.

"Know that I trust you two more than words can say." With that, he opened the door wide and swept his arm before him.

Nick jerked to a stop at the sight of the woman who snapped to her feet. The resemblance to Marvin was striking—the firm determination etched in her face, those snapping blue eyes. Light brown hair was caught in a ponytail that swung to her shoulders. She wore a dark blue T-shirt that hugged her curves and accentuated her full breasts, while not being too indiscreet. Her jeans also complemented her assets, but didn't bind. Black boots capped off the attire.

Nick could almost feel her heart pound...or was that his? He dared a step forward, wanting to smell her, see those eyes close up. Her gaze locked to his, refusing to back down. He liked that...a lot.

Marvin shut the door with a resounding thud. "Gentlemen, my daughter Gabrielle. Gaby, Nick and Reid. I'm sure both are familiar to you. They will be *guiding* you in this endeavor."

So that confirmed the relationship Nick suspected. He wasn't sure what surprised him more: that Marvin actually had a child, or hearing next that Gaby was a cop. The real shocker came with the subsequent news. Nick's skin crawled to know one of their own was preying on women.

"Gaby's come for my help infiltrating one of the private clubs to catch this man." Marvin clearly wasn't happy about it either. Each word came out through almost clenched teeth.

Nick knew exactly how he felt.

"To my knowledge, she's a novice when it comes to our lifestyle. Is that still so?"

Nick glanced up in time to see Marvin glaring down his nose at his daughter.

She held her own with him. "Yes, Dad."

Nick drew a breath to protest. Reid beat him to it.

"I must question the sanity of such an action."

Marvin snorted. "She's my daughter, through and through, and determined. She's her mother's daughter, too—stubborn to a fault. She's going in whether I help her or not." He took a position between Gaby and them. "That's where the two of you come in. Teach her. Make sure she's fully indoctrinated on all aspects of what she's set on doing. I don't want anyone making her for a fraud. And when I say everything, I mean everything. Her old rooms are at the other end of the hall, ready and waiting as they always are for her. Anything you need to help"—he spread his palms out—"is yours. You know how well-stocked the facility is. I'll advise the staff you're to be accommodated."

He jerked around to Gaby and cupped her chin in a loose grip. The sternness in his eyes softened. "She's the love of my life. The princess of my heart, conceived by the grace of God when a condom failed. The minute she was born I had a vasectomy because I knew no other child in the world would ever compare, could ever match the love I have for her."

Tears momentarily puddled in Gaby's blue eyes. She rapidly blinked them away.

Marvin dropped his hand and faced them with a sigh. "I trust you both with her life. I trust you both to help keep her safe. See she learns her lessons well. If you have to dress her up and trot her around downstairs, do so. Allow no one—no one—down there to touch her. Once she's ready, I'll see she's invited to whatever club her people have targeted. I'd prefer you both accompany her, if possible. I know it's a lot to ask, but I want experienced hands at her back. I'll be out of touch for the remainder of the evening."

And just like that, he left.

The three of them stood there, strangers thrust into a scene none of them expected. Nick and Reid were getting a lot of that tonight. He couldn't speak for Reid, but Nick wasn't sure how easily he could roll into this. Gaby Keating…intrigued him. And here he thought his cock was down for the night. Nothing like getting a second wind.

Nick moved closer. His fingers itched to touch her. "It might be best if we took this to your room to discuss and evaluate matters. You might find that once you have a fuller understanding of what happens in these clubs you'll change your mind."

Her chin came up a notch. "Women are being tortured and murdered. Nothing will make me change my mind."

Reid crossed his arms and stared down at her. "The burning heat of a leather strap across your bare ass could make you change your mind quickly."

Gaby's cheeks flushed. For the first time since they'd walked into the room, her gaze dropped. "Whatever it takes," she muttered.

"When had you planned to go under?" Reid asked.

She forced her eyes upward once more. "As soon as possible."

"Then we're in for a long night." Nick cupped her elbow and steered her toward the door.

She didn't budge.

Nick grabbed her other elbow. "First lesson…you are the sub, we are the Doms. Don't balk, don't dawdle, do what we say when we say it or we're all screwed."

Gaby moved then.

Nick wrapped his arm around her shoulders. She smelled of rich chocolate. His body watered for a taste. "Your father trusts us with your welfare. Now you have to trust in that, too." He dropped his hand to her firm ass. "Now, come. We need to spend some time getting comfortable with each other." He was half tempted to add a solid swat to punctuate the sentence, but Nick had a feeling she'd fist his balls a second later, and not in a good way.

She eyed the tray of food on the end table, devoid of all but fruit, sandwiches, and one lonely piece of fudge. Nick picked it up and brought it to her lips. Gaby hesitated, then opened her mouth and bit off half. Nick grinned and took the other.

"Ah, shit," Reid groaned. "Here we go again."

Gaby glanced from one to the other. "What does that mean?" she asked around the mouthful of chocolate.

"It means he's being a smart ass." Nick motioned her forward. "Your rooms?"

"This way."

Nick watched her ass the whole way down the hall, his cock getting harder and harder with every step.

*   *   *

Nick Tristan in the flesh, and way better looking than Gaby had ever imagined. She could still feel the heat of his talented hand pressed against her butt. It spread down to her crotch, swelling her against the seam of her jeans. Every Mesquite lyric she'd ever memorized now sounded like it was made for her, especially those that came from Nick's lips. She felt like some sappy teenager caught in a crush of an elusive rock star. But here he was, one half of the testosterone-laden duo who were her entry into *that* world, the keys to catching a killer.

She and Reid had crossed paths at the courthouse over the years—he as an attorney, she as a witness. Though they'd never spoken directly or even in the context of their respective professions, Gaby admired Reid's work ethic. Others spoke highly of him. Little did she realize when they'd exchanged polite nods in passing that they would be in this position. Trust him? Until the comment about strapping her ass, yes. Now?

She forced herself to stay on course. Gaby knew she'd suffer far worse going undercover without some experience, and the fact her father asked Nick and Reid to go with her calmed her immensely. Her father trusted these men. She trusted her father.

"Please tell me we aren't walking into pink ruffles and a white canopy bed," Reid said.

Gaby rolled her gaze upward, making sure they both saw it. "Puleese. Do I look like a Disney princess to either of you?"

Nick's hand found her rear again. "If you frequently go undercover, I'd imagine you can be whatever you choose for the occasion."

Gaby didn't bother to tell him this would be her first undercover assignment. Brass wasn't too thrilled with the idea, but there were few other options available. Her father could get her in. He might not be so inclined with another officer. Hell, he wasn't inclined with her, just cornered. Gaby didn't want to imagine what repercussions were in store. Maybe he'd given Nick and Reid private instructions to wear her ass out. The thought didn't set well, made her edgy and unsure. She'd had her spills, knocks, bumps, and bruises, but she'd never been physically punished. Not so much as a hand swat over either of her parent's knees.

"Maybe we could use 'princess' as a sub name for you."

Gaby's glare at Nick told him they'd better not try. To her annoyance, he merely chuckled. She hurried ahead to throw the door open on her suite of rooms, then wanted to die on the spot. The décor was green and cream with plush furnishings dying to embrace one's body. But the hint of sophistication was washed away by her treasured collection of stuffed animals all lined up on the sofa where she'd left them six months ago. Heat swamped her face. She braced herself for the inevitable snide male comments.

Silence…and then the door clicked shut behind her.

"Need help putting them away?" Nick asked. "If it helps, I still have my collection of Matchbox cars."

"Me, too," Reid added. "I…uhm…have been known to play with them from time to time."

"Oh, yeah. Line them all up with my Star Wars action figures."

Gaby couldn't help laughing. Talk about a great icebreaker. "Thanks, guys. Yes, a little help would be nice. There's a walk-in closet in the bedroom."

The men cradled her stuffed friends with care. Nick even smiled when he lifted her favorite bunny, ears bare of fuzz from years of loving.

"Why here and not in your own home?" he asked.

"I don't have a good answer," she admitted. "Maybe this room feels more like home than my apartment."

"Sounds like an answer to me," Reid said, then gave her a knowing look from under his eyebrows as he picked up more animals.

"Yes, I suppose it is." Odd she hadn't realized it until now. Maybe that was why she hadn't bothered nesting in her place.

She darted ahead of their trek to the bedroom to make sure no strays were in residence there. The full-size bed was clear of everything except a couple of big pillows. The men respected her boundaries at the closet and handed the stuffed toys to her to place where she wanted. Gaby noticed both of them scoping out the room. She would have done the same if their situations were reversed. Once they were finished, the three of them returned to the living area. Awkwardness settled in. Should she sit? Kneel before them? What?

"I'm not good at being submissive," she said.

"We sorta noticed," Nick replied. "But then, isn't dominance an edge you need in your line of work?"

He didn't give her a chance to respond.

"It might surprise you—but again it might not—that there are many people who are dominant in their day jobs, yet submissive in their other activities."

"So I understand." Her mother was a bank executive, a very demanding job. And yet when asked, she'd told Gaby she preferred a submissive role in her afterhours. She'd never met a stronger woman than her mother.

"I presume you know about safe words?" Nick asked.

"I do." Her heart was thumping a mile a minute. It paled in comparison to her clit, which now thudded against a suddenly too-tight crotch seam.

"Have you ever been spanked?" Reid asked.

God help her, the thought moistened her panties, while it scared the hell out of her. "Never," she managed to reply.

"How soon do you anticipate us going under?" Nick asked.

Us. So, they'd agreed. Now, would her department agree to them going with her? "Within days."

He and Reid rubbed their chins and passed gazes up and down her body. "Find a way to stain her skin?" Reid asked.

Nick nodded. "I'm sure George has stuff in the kitchen we can use."

Gaby frowned. "You've lost me."

Nick snagged the bottom of her T-shirt. "If you're going to be a well-used sub, you're going to have to look the part. We'll make up your body so it'll look like you've been whipped and paddled thoroughly. We're certainly not going to do that to you."

Her knees quaked. When Nick started to tug her T-shirt up, she snatched it back down.

"Off," he ordered. "Or you *will* be spanked."

But he just said... Why were her nipples so damn hard?

"There's only so much we can fake, Gaby." His thumb brushed over her bare stomach. Her body clenched with want. "We have to get used to being naked around each other."

"We're also going to have to have sex."

She jerked her head to Reid. "All three of us?"

Reid pulled the elastic band from her hair, then combed his fingers through it. Her body leaned into Nick, breasts craving the feel of his hard chest.

"We might be required to do so at the club. You don't want any surprises." Nick slid the T-shirt up, brushing his fingers over her hard nipples through her bra. She could just as well have been naked. The feeling was electric.

Reid pressed against her back, wedging her between them. They were both hard, big men. *How in the hell...*

Nick whipped the T-shirt over her head. Instinctively, her hand slid over his shoulders to draw him nearer. She pressed her ass against Reid. He unbuttoned her fly, unzipped, and tugged her jeans down. Gaby flinched. Nick's hot hand slipped into her panties and spanned her butt cheek. The jeans came down the rest of the way. Her boots trapped them at her ankles. Her panties followed. Nick slid his fingers between her slick labia. Gaby arched into Reid and lost her bra a second later. Her boots bound her in place. Reid twirled her nipples between his fingers. Nick rocked her clit under a relentless caress.

"We're going to make you come." Nick's voice rumbled against her ear. "Then you're going to get your first spanking."

She squeezed her thighs around the hand wedged between them. "No, please." Cream trickled down her thighs.

"I saw a hairbrush on the dresser." Nick pinched her clit. "Not wooden, but it'll do. Reid, could you get it now? One orgasm and she's over my knee. It'd be cruel to make her wait."

"My pleasure." He thrust his erection against her, then left.

Gaby shook her head. "No, no, please don't."

Nick nailed her ass in place with one hand, while the other worked her clit and thrust into her pussy. She was coming. God help her, she was coming! Gaby fought it, knowing that with the climax she'd find herself facedown over Nick's lap. And still she humped his hand.

He traced the cleft of her butt cheeks, delving toward the hole in back. And orgasm burst free. She shook with the force, then sagged in his arms. An instant later she was looking at the gray-green carpet. She gasped with the feel of the cool hairbrush rubbing over her ass.

Gaby squirmed for freedom, hair tumbling over her face, blinding her. "No, no, no!"

Reid squatted down to her level, raked her hair into his fist, and pulled her head up gently. "In this world, no doesn't mean no. You say no and you're going to get it. Think, Gaby. Focus. What do you say when you really mean no."

She'd just had a blinding orgasm, so how could she focus on anything?

"Safe word, Gaby, or you're going to feel it good." Nick tapped her ass with the brush.

Her clit swelled into the barely-there hit. She wanted and didn't want. She'd never been so conflicted.

"This isn't a game, princess," Nick added. "This is life and death. There's no time to play."

The words sank into her haze. "Red light," she gasped out.

Both men released her.

"Good girl." Nick turned her until he could cradle her in his arms. Reid moved to her feet and removed the boots.

Nick caressed her side, dotting kisses to her forehead. "Now…you and I are going to take a shower while Reid scrounges what we need."

Gaby cuddled against his shoulder, then nodded. She doubted her heartbeat would ever return to normal. The rush of adrenaline was…sweet.

CHAPTER 3

Nick loved how Gaby had come so quickly under his hand. Her juices drenched him, her scent oozing into his pores. *So beautiful. So perfect. So trusting.* Too trusting, considering the situation into which she was about to enter. His duty was to see she was informed and protected. Under any other circumstance he'd consider her trust a treasured gift. But not now when her life depended on him teaching her all he could in the short span of a day or two.

It scared the hell out of him. He wanted to bask in her, to spend hours, days, weeks, months learning her body over and over again. To memorize the feel of her pussy clenched around his cock. To feel her lips surround him, her fingers cupping his balls while she did so. And maybe…just maybe…to earn enough of her real trust to take it all to a higher level.

He waited until Reid left, then helped her stand. Her legs quivered, threatening to topple her. He didn't know if it was because of passion or fear, and he wasn't about to ask. Gaby had to be the best she could be, at top form for this assignment. If he had to make her come a thousand times to settle her into the job, he'd do it, even at the expense of his own balls bursting.

He wanted to love on her, not play the Dom/sub game. Still…it was about survival.

"When we're in that situation, you have to obey without question." He cleared his throat. "The slightest hesitation will tell. You don't leave our sides. Lean into us at all times. Eyes downcast. No speaking until you're given permission to do so. You'll address us both as 'Master,' nothing else. If you disregard any of those things, I'll have no choice but to discipline you."

She shivered. All Nick wanted to do was wrap his arms around her.

"Unbutton my shirt, princess."

Gaby stood before him, eyes focused on her task, breath wafting over his skin as she slowly bared him. She pressed her lips together at her first glimpse of his chest and started to reach for his nipple. She paused, fingers hovering over her goal. Sweet blue eyes glanced up at him.

"May I touch you…Master?"

"Very good, Gaby. That's exactly correct."

"Good. So…may I?"

Hell, yeah. "Yes, you may."

She bent down and flicked her tongue over the bead of flesh. He felt the shock in his balls and sucked in a breath through his teeth.

"Damn it, Gaby." He stabbed his hand in her hair and pulled back her head. "I didn't say with your tongue."

"You didn't say not to either," she purred.

She had him on that one. "You have a boyfriend?"

Gaby drew back. A tiny line marked the space between her eyebrows. "Do you think if I did I'd be doing this with you?" She hooked her foot behind his leg, and he knew she intended to flip him.

"Do it and no safe word in the world will save your ass."

War backlit her gaze. The choice was hers. Nick meant what he said. Finally, she dropped her gaze and released the last two buttons.

"Good." He took a step backward and pressed his hands to her shoulders. "On your knees. I presume you're familiar with the position."

Defiance reared its head again. "What—"

"The submissive position, not doggy style position, or standing on your head."

Gaby knelt and placed her hands on her thighs, eyes downcast.

"Now…unzip my trousers and release my cock. Don't touch it…with any part of your body or anything else."

He sensed her anger growing by the second. Gaby was a strong, dominant woman. He'd be lucky if she didn't snap off his dick and shove it up his ass, then use his testicles to shoot pool.

"It's very likely you'll have to do this in front of others, Gaby." Maybe the reasoning would calm her. "Reid and I will do our best to prevent it, but if this man makes contact, you could very well find yourself in that situation."

Her shoulders lifted on a deep breath, like she was centering herself, reinforcing her resolve. She eased open the fly button, then slowly pulled down the zipper. Long fingers reached for his erection, then hesitated.

"Through the boxers, Master, or completely down?"

He swallowed the knot that suddenly formed in his throat. God, she was beautiful, lips a breath away from his crotch. "Down," he managed to say.

She wrapped her fingers in the waistband and tugged.

"Raise up," he said. "Closer. I want to feel my cock fall between those gorgeous breasts."

He watched her nipples harden all the more. Lips pressed together, then the tip of her tongue licked them apart. She brushed her breasts against his thighs, her cheek against the erection, then moved up until her mouth touched his navel. Trousers and boxers slid free. She gasped when his erection freed. Eyes closed, lips parted. She shoved the clothing downward and brushed her fingers up the backs of his thighs. Upper arms squeezed her breasts into a deep cleavage that wrapped around his penis.

Nick gasped and cupped her head. Her breath heated the tip of his cock. He glanced down; blue fire looked up at him. As her Dom, he knew he could demand she suck him, but…

"If it was just me and you, no agenda, what would you do right now, princess?" he asked softly.

"I'd swallow your beautiful cock whole," she replied without hesitation.

"You may…indulge." He could barely get the words out.

"Thank you…Master," she whispered, and closed her lips around his cock.

His knees buckled. Body trembled. She dug her short nails into his ass and licked him from tip to root and back again. He pumped into her mouth with the vigor of a virgin sixteen-year-old, not the seasoned grace of a well-trained Dom. Her tongue felt like wildfire, quick and hot, engulfing him before he could catch a good breath. It wasn't enough.

Nick wanted her under him, over him. Wanted to be buried so deep inside her that a nuclear blast couldn't rip them apart. Breasts rasped against his thighs, hard nipples furrowing the hair there, implanting seeds he knew would erupt passion in his deepest dreams. He tried to rein in control, to keep his thrusts shallow. Each time, Gaby sucked him so deep Nick swore he felt her vocal chords.

Balls hugged his body and tried to crawl out his cock and into the pleasure of her mouth. He couldn't hold back and didn't want to. They might be facing life and death reality soon, but soon wasn't now. He could lose control, let her suck him dry if that's what she wanted.

Gaby's groan hummed along his dick. Sparkles burst behind his eyes. He felt like an animal rutting, and growled like one, too. Hips snapped forward, muscles locked with tension, and every ounce of fluid in his body shot from him. Gaby gulped it down, easing the pressure as the sensation waned. She didn't let go until he grew flaccid and then released him slowly with kisses against his cock, balls, and groin.

Nick didn't know how his legs still held him. He was conscious of petting her hair, of the warmth glowing inside and swelling his heart. Now he knew how his brothers felt. Trouble was, Nick didn't have a clue where to go from here.

Shower, his conscience nudged. He found himself nodding in reply.

Catching her arms, he gently tugged her to her feet. "There's a shower calling our names."

She rested her head against his shoulder. "Are you pleased, Master?"

The term soured his stomach. He wanted *his* name on her lips, not that of a role he sometimes assumed.

"Very much so, sweetheart." He kissed her forehead, rubbed her ass, and turned them toward the bathroom.

* * *

Sweetheart. Gaby couldn't remember when she'd ever heard the endearment uttered with so much reverence. Tucked under Nick's arm as he led them to the shower, nothing felt more right. Emotions skipped around her. She felt…giddy, light-headed—and it wasn't from the killer orgasm. Something else was going on here.

Probably a crash from the sugar rush.

Gaby ignored her internal nag. She knew her feelings weren't part of the scene, but she sure as hell wasn't going to pick it apart to analyze right now. Unfortunately, she didn't have time to savor the moment either.

She placed her hand on his chest. "Let me put out an extra set of towels."

"I'll get the water hot."

He kissed her then, short and sweet, but with so much affection all the chocolate in the world couldn't compete. Her heart tumbled into her stomach and bounced back up again. Butterflies, rainbows, and sunbeams. And here she thought her life was nothing but collars, perps, and victims.

She pulled the towel set from the small linen closet and clutched it to her chest as she watched his silhouette behind the glass shower door. Sculptors carved monuments to men with bodies like his, but no work of art she'd ever seen matched Nick's attributes. He took care of his body, too. She'd seen cops who spent half their lives working out and didn't look a quarter as fit.

Gaby laughed to herself. Other than the penis wedged against her back, she'd paid little attention to Reid at all. And that was just fine with her. She'd apparently found what she was looking for. Whether Nick "found" her back...well, she'd worry about that later.

"I've never showered with someone else before." She draped the towels over the bar and tossed the washcloth over the top of the door for him. He snagged it mid-air. "Unless you count other women at the gym or academy."

Nick froze. "Uhm...yeah...it counts...in my fantasies."

"I thought it might." Gaby grinned. She twisted her hair and secured it on top of her head with one of the barrettes she kept in the vanity drawer. "I won't destroy the illusion by telling you nothing happened."

"Thanks. But maybe you could embellish the tale into visions of grand orgies and girl-on-girl action?"

Gaby's grin widened. She really liked this guy...in more ways than one. "I'll think about it," she said with a laugh and opened the door.

Damn, he was gorgeous. A perfect peach-shaped ass, narrow waist that fanned up into broad chest and shoulders, a light smattering of chest hair that darkened the lower it went and pointed the way to nirvana. Even at rest his cock looked yummy and tempted her to see how quickly she could awaken it.

Gaby yanked her wandering attention to a halt. She was here to prepare for a job, not indulge her lust. "So, what's the purpose of showering together? I do know my way around a handheld shower, by the way."

Nick lifted an eyebrow her way. "You're killing me, you know that?"

"Don't worry. I use my powers for good, not evil." She twisted her washcloth and snapped his ass.

Nick gasped and grabbed her wrist. A hot gaze devoured her, weakened her knees, and churned the juices in her crotch. "Be careful what you start, princess." He yanked her close, his semi-hard penis between them, and gave her a sharp whack on the ass.

"Ow!" She glowered at him, despite the fire racing to her pussy.

"Life and death, Gaby," he said. "Yours, mine, and Reid's. I honestly don't think you can pull this off. You're too much a dominant. That quality oozes from your pores."

She drew breath to defend herself. Nick snapped his palm up to stop her.

"Point one…I find that quality very attractive. Not that it matters to you, I'm sure. I have women throwing themselves at me constantly. That rush wore off years ago. In this environment, the women want to take a submissive role, and while it's enticing, that rush, too, is fading. There's no substance. It's sex by rote. You are substance."

How did she respond to that? What exactly was he saying? He was getting her emotions off-track again, setting her heartbeat to thudding against her ribs. He had to feel it racing since there wasn't enough space between them for a water drop.

"Point two," he said. "Your dominance fits you well in your job. You have to be strong and confident. This is an undercover job, just like any other you've ever done. You have to be the person you say you are. This isn't scoring a drug buy or playing a hooker. This is hunting down a killer. One slip and we're all dead."

Gaby tore her gaze away from him so he wouldn't see the lie in her eyes. He caught her chin and forced her to look at him.

"Oh, my God! You've never done this before!"

Too late. Caught and hoisted. Gaby couldn't muster a denial.

Nick grabbed her shoulders and gave her a little shake. "Have you lost your mind? Does your department even know you're doing this?"

"Of course they know," she snapped. At least she'd found her voice. "Do you think I'd risk not sending this guy to jail because I fucked up a collar and didn't go by procedure?"

He loosened his hold and put a few inches between them. "And yet you're willing to wind up in the morgue."

Gaby placed her palm against his broad chest and closed the gap. "Nick, that's my job. I'm at risk every time I put on that uniform, every time I go out on the street."

He closed his eyes and turned his head away. His shoulders rose and fell on slow, measured breaths. Finally, he looked at her once more, hands fisted loosely at his sides.

"Perhaps it would be best if we trained your partner to go in with you."

Gaby scrunched her face. "Ewww. I don't want Nestor seeing me naked. And I sure as hell don't want to see that bear of a man nude. Never mind the fact he's married and his wife would kill him."

Nick's grin was back. "I think you managed to knock the girl-on-girl shower scenes out of my head." Just as quickly his humor faded. "Then, my lead from this point on. If you don't, I will purposefully sabotage your efforts by spreading the word throughout the community of what you're trying to do. By the time I'm finished, you won't be allowed on the same block as one of those clubs, much less over the threshold."

Now that pissed her off. "You'd let a murderer go free?" If she was in a better position, she'd clutch his balls in a vice-like grip that would have him blubbering like a baby.

Nick caught her wrists and hauled them over her head, as if he'd anticipated her intent. "Princess"—he nailed her wrists against the tile wall with one hand and slid the other down her body—"I'd do whatever it takes to keep you alive. Understood?"

When she didn't answer, merely glared, he swooped his hand to her breast and tweaked her nipple. "Understood?"

God help her, she gasped and arched into him. She clamped her lips tight, determined to win. Nick moved so quickly it made her head spin. Gaby found herself draped over his thigh, her ass in the air. Her wrists were captured in his steely grip at her lower back.

"Gabrielle..." His voice warned her. The cool plastic brushing over her ass added more weight. He'd grabbed the shower brush.

Her heartbeat roared in her ears. Her skin tingled from the shower spray. She lifted her legs to brace against the wall and shove him off balance. Again, Nick anticipated the move and sank to the bottom of the stall. He locked his legs around hers and anchored her hands to her lower back.

Gaby squirmed until she was in biting distance.

"Do it and I swear I'll tie you to the bed and give you a strapping you'll never forget."

"You wouldn't dare. I'll have you arrested for assaulting a police officer."

Nick rolled her over, wedging the shower brush between her legs. "And what are you going to do when we go under, Gaby? When the choice is to take a spanking or give up your cover? You learn to take it now, just like you learn to be comfortable with me and Reid. Like you learn to be comfortable with the sex. Trust me, you'll be dealing with enough surprises. Let's handle those we can anticipate now."

The fight went out of her. Nick had a very valid point. "Understood," she replied, her voice soft, and rolled facedown.

Nick's hold loosened. He rubbed his hand over her ass, then followed with the brush bristles over her bottom, down her thighs and up the insides. Gaby parted her legs for more.

"Know that I never give punishment spankings unless a women specifically requests it, princess," he said, nestling the brush against her clit. "I don't care for them. I'm all about the pleasure. Between the two of us—the three of us, I suppose—I can make it look like you got the beating of your life. That illusion will save our skins."

"So...you were bluffing now?" She peeked over her shoulder.

"Perhaps yes, perhaps no." He flipped the brush and rubbed the back into position over her ass. "Odd that not once did you utter a safe word."

"God *damn* you—"

A solid whack cut her off. Gaby swallowed a protest. It stung and burned...but not only in the places she'd anticipated. She lay across his lap, shower spray beating down on them, waiting, wanting. An erection swelled against her hip. His knee found its way to her crotch and wedged in. Gaby's pussy lips kissed it.

"Your pussy is hot, sweetheart. Your clit hard as a pebble. Everything is swollen and ready to come. And I promise you, it'll feel damn good when you do. Hold onto the feeling; let it warm and absorb you. You might need to draw on it later."

"Am I...going to have to do with this Reid, too?"

"Over my dead body." He rubbed the brush over her bottom, then landed another smack.

Gaby groaned and clenched her thighs around his knee. "Are you going to spank me until I come?"

"Am I...or will I?" he asked.

Gaby swallowed another groan with the next smack and rocked into his knee. "Will you?" she gasped. "Please."

"I will." Two more smacks rained down.

Hands braced against the bottom of the stall, she arched into the spanking. With each stroke she rode him harder, wishing she could get his knee inside her pussy. Nick was slow, methodical, building the fire higher and higher as he covered every inch of her backside. He let her hump his knee, matching her groans with phrases that fired her up all the more.

That's it, baby.

Fuck me.

Make yourself come.

Let it go.

Feel the rise.

Sweet, isn't it?

"God, Nick," she gasped. "I never…"

"But aren't you so glad you did?" The bristles ran down her thighs and back up. "Come, sweetheart. And after you do, I'm going to carry you to your bed and taste your sweet pussy, make you come all over again. And then I'm going to fuck you. Feel how hard my dick is?"

"Yes," she cried out, and groaned and rolled with another smack.

"Imagine how it'll feel clenched inside you."

"Yes," she gasped. "Oh, yes!" She could imagine it very, very well. "Nick…I… Oh, Nick!"

He spanked her through the rolling orgasm that shook her body. She slumped over his lap, sated and spent. He braced her against him, rubbing bath oil over her warmed bottom, dipping his fingers into her ass, promising with his touch what his words had told her would happen next. Gaby let him play, let him explore her, content in his arms, safe, wanting so much that she couldn't put into words.

She scooted until she was astride his hips and that glorious cock tucked into the natural cleft of her body. Lips parted, she leaned in. Nick's mouth covered hers without hesitation. Hands spanned against her back pulled her closer until her breasts were crushed into his chest. It still wasn't close enough.

His kiss touched her from head to toe and everywhere between. Thorough, demanding, yet somehow tempered. Like he wanted to lay her out and pound into her, but was determined to tame the cave-beast in him…barely. One shift and he'd impale her. Neither of them let the rising passion overtake their senses.

Nick pulled his lips from hers, but the kiss continued in the look as his eyes passed over her face. Holding her close, he stood, with her legs wrapped around his waist.

"Turn off the water, baby," he said.

A twist of her wrist followed through. A second later he opened the shower door.

Nick set her onto the bathmat and snagged a towel from the bar. He blotted her dry, gaze admiring what lay hidden under the water drops. Then he unclipped her damp hair and did the same there before wrapping the towel around her and grabbing the second one. She expected he'd scuff the towel over himself. Instead, he handed it to her.

Gaby shivered. The things he did to her body, her heart. Most men were in, out, and gone by breakfast. No one took time for more. No one took time to…make love. Crazy as it sounded, she knew that's what Nick was doing. This wasn't about her learning anything. This was about a man wanting a woman, wanting her.

She danced the towel over his body, wondering if the water cried out at having to be parted from him. Gaby knew she would. She hated the distance now and it was mere inches.

She glanced down at his cock, full, proud, and hard. Droplets clung to his dark pubic hair. She wanted them on her, wanted their bodies linked. Hungered to feel him spreading her wide and making her his.

"I'm going to carry you to your bed now, princess."

His low voice pierced her fog.

"No condoms." She shook her head and tried to clarify. "I have none."

"I have one," he said. "Reid will bring more."

The other man's name hit her cold. Gaby flinched. Nick cupped her neck and kissed her. "I don't like it either…now. I don't like anything you're planning to do. But I will do anything and everything to make sure you're safe, Gaby. Even share you with another man if that saves your life."

She closed her eyes against tears and sank into his kiss. How could she have fallen so hard, so fast, for a man she'd just met? But she sure as hell didn't deny the emotion. Apparently Nick didn't either. She broke the kiss and butted her forehead against his.

"I love a man who doesn't play games."

Nick kneaded her butt. "And I love a strong woman who knows what she wants."

"I want you, Nick," she said in a rush of breath.

"I want you, too. I *need* you."

He scooped her into his arms. Gaby bit back a protest that she was too heavy. Nick Tristan could do anything, and if he wanted to carry her to the ends of the universe and back, she'd let him. She rested her head against his shoulder, feeling very much a princess as he carried her into her old bedroom. He placed her in the middle of the full-size bed with little effort, then covered her body with his and sealed their lips.

She hooked her legs around his and writhed into him. Nick moaned and deepened the kiss, thrusting his erection against her belly.

He yanked his head up. “God, I could fuck your belly button.”

Before Gaby could respond, he latched onto her neck, kneading the tender muscle up and down with his lips. She released what little control she possessed, gliding her fingers through his wet hair and cradling his head. Her body felt more alive than it had in years. His touch was beyond any adrenaline rush. Lips and fingers ignited her core, yet still managed to raise goose bumps along her skin. The contradiction made her laugh. Mouth suckling her nipples changed it to a moan he repeated.

“How can you keep from fucking me?” The words came out a whimpered plea.

Nick lifted his head, dark brown eyes burning. “It’s not easy. Knowing I’m seconds away from tasting your pussy makes the wait worth it.”

He crawled down her body, licking, nipping, pausing long enough to twirl his tongue into the well of her navel and make her writhe. Then he cupped her hips and wiggled lower. His shoulders nudged between her thighs, silently demanding she draped her legs over them.

Gaby stared down, knowing the hunger in his eyes matched her own. His breath tickled her pubic hair. “Am I pretty there?”

Nick glanced at her pussy. “Absolutely beautiful.” And then his tongue dove into her pussy.

Gaby jerked into the caress, balling the thick bedspread in one hand, while she grasped his head with the other.

“That’s it, sweetheart,” he said, “fuck my face.” He dove in again, gliding his tongue through parts of her Gaby never imagined could be erogenous. And ignoring the one part of her she knew was.

He milked her labia. Traced the valleys and peaks. Licked her cream. Mindless pleas tore from her throat, begging him “More,” and “Please,” and “Oh, yes!” Grunts responded, firing her up all the more. Gaby couldn’t bear the wait, but never wanted it to end. Then his fingers found her anus, and his thumb tunneled into her pussy. She clamped onto him, quivering because she knew what he’d do next.

A wall-shattering moan left her mouth when his lips closed over her clit. He suckled gently, teasing the climax to him while he finger-fucked her hard. Thinking of his cock inside, knowing how great he could make her come…

Gaby couldn't catch her breath, couldn't think beyond the swelling below. Each flick of his tongue urged her higher, each nibble of his lips drew the sensation out. She jerked upright as best she could, shoving his mouth right where she needed it.

Nick glanced up, face wet from her juices. "Not have enough spanking?"

A flush heated her body. She flopped back down and spread her legs wide.

"What will it be next time, sweetheart?" His thumb danced over her clit. "Wooden hairbrush, paddle, a belt? Remember how it felt to come under a spanking?"

She did! God, she did! And wanted it.

"Imagine dildos in your pussy and ass. Vibrating away, while that pretty little bottom gets hotter and hotter and your clit swells to bursting."

Gaby whimpered and wiggled under him. The words and images they spawned were enough to make her come. *So close. So close.*

"I want to make you come, Gaby. But you feel like a furnace. Do you know how much my cock wants inside you? I know the ache is bad. Mine is, too. I want to feel you come around me. Can you do that, sweetheart? Can you wait long enough for me?"

Emotion clawed for freedom. "Yes, Nick. Yes! Please. I need you inside. That's exactly what I need."

He eased his fingers from her and dropped a kiss to her clit. "I promise I'll be right back. Keep your fingers away from this jewel until I get back."

"Or you'll spank me for coming without you? Right?" She couldn't believe the words came out of her mouth.

"That's right, baby. Enough to make you come a thousand times more."

She griped the bedspread and counted the seconds until he returned. Gaby could barely see him through the door. Her heart ached for the loss of view. Her body chilled. Nick was back in less than a minute, engorged cock fully sheathed and sniffing her out.

He crawled onto the bed between her open legs. Gaby reached for him and he fell into her arms. Gazes locked, heartbeats thudding against each other, he seated himself in a solid thrust.

They sucked in a simultaneous breath and held it for what seemed eternity before letting it out. He felt like magic...like love. She feathered her hands over his shoulders, down his back, memorizing everything about him. It wasn't that he filled her body. Nick filled her heart.

He combed tendrils of her hair away from her face, then lifted her arm and brought her fingers to his lips. He kissed each one before he sucked them into his mouth one at a time. And when he'd completed the circuit, Nick shoved her hand between them right to her clit.

"It's gonna be quick," she warned him.

He grinned. "Yeah, real quick."

She pressed her clit into him. Nick's eyes rolled a second before bliss closed them. Gaby wanted to watch the pleasure absorb him when he came. His thrust cancelled any thought but them reaching the goal together. She nailed her heels into his ass, absorbing every pounding stroke he slammed into her and demanding more, more, more.

Her bed creaked under the impact. Sex sounds bounced off the walls and beyond, surely rivaling anything coming from anyone else tonight. Gaby loved his stamina, the feel of his weight on her, his muscles flexing in time with hers.

"Damn, you're tight," he spit out.

"Damn...you're hard," she managed to reply. "You're...perfect."

Nick's eyes flashed open, jaw clenched. "And you're mine." He pushed hard, grinding against her. "Come, Gaby. Come now. I can't hold out much longer." He pushed even deeper, dragging her clit with him.

Gaby let go, grappling for his shoulders as if it could bring them closer. His cock felt like steel, molten hot steel. "I never want to let go. I want to fuck you forever."

Nick's groan rumbled through his chest. His body shook from the effort to hold on for her. Gaby nudged his lips with hers. He shook his head, then gave in and clamped his mouth over hers. Tongues flailed, then froze. Muscles locked. They jerked lips apart on a simultaneous cry and exploded in what had to be *the* best orgasm of Gaby's life.

Nick stabbed a few shallow strokes into her, then plunged in deep again. Then again. Until the moment ebbed and they lay panting in each other's arms.

Words. Something as wondrous as this deserved words. Gaby let gentle kisses and long caresses over his shoulders say with her touch what she couldn't utter.

Nick remained quiet as well, combing her hair, dropping kisses to her cheeks and neck until their heartbeats slowed to normal. Then he drew breath to say something.

Reid's return brought reality crashing down. "I'm back. Sorry it took so long. You two ready to do this?"

"Yeah…sure." The look Nick gave her contradicted him. "Whatever it takes to keep you safe. Understood?"

Gaby nodded. "Understood."

CHAPTER 4

"How do you feel?" Nick brushed his hands down her bound arms.

Gaby glanced over her shoulder at him. "Like a specimen on display."

He and Reid had tied her spread-eagle in the doorway. Soft leather cuffs surrounded her ankles and wrists. Nothing was left to anyone's imagination. The position was necessary for them to get their body marks correct when they painted her. The stain would wear off eventually.

"It might come to that once we're there." Reid stirred a small paintbrush in a little cup.

His scavenger hunt in George's kitchen had apparently netted him gold. He'd returned with enough food coloring, paintbrushes, and assorted mixing cups to paint the entire house. He'd also paid little attention to her body since he walked back into the room and found her and Nick in bed. He respected Nick's unspoken rights. Gaby liked that about Reid. Liked him even more for ducking into the shower to give them extra minutes to recover. That helped now. He studied her with the eye of a gem cutter, wondering where to strike first.

He cocked his head to one side, gaze on her crotch. "The pubic hair needs to go."

"No," Nick said before she could utter a word. "This man's going to want a challenge. I noticed from the crime scene photos he targeted areas with hair. If she has none, that'll make her less tempting. He wants the lure of burning the hair off."

Gaby lifted her eyebrow. "You're a profiler now?"

Nick checked her circulation in hands and feet. "Knowledge is power. I've tried to learn all I can about everything. The entertainment world is a fickle mistress. I like to be prepared for when we're no longer at the top of the charts." He shrugged a shoulder. "Maybe even turn to writing."

She snickered. "Talk about a fickle mistress."

He grinned. "Yeah, but it'll give the voices in my head an outlet."

"Where in the world are your people going to hide a wire?" Reid question jolted her.

"I…I'm sure they'll figure something out."

"Hmm… Ever had anal sex?" Reid asked.

She felt her body flush with heat. "Yes."

"Good. There won't be any way we can fake it if we get in that situation." He set the cup down and prepared another. "The best we can do tonight is learn one another so we can function better as a team."

"And what *will* we be able to fake?"

Nick wrapped his hand around the flogger Reid had purloined from the basement playrooms. "Whipping. I'll be controlling the follow-through to ease the stroke, but you'll need to time the perfect reaction to it or they'll know we're faking."

He ducked under her arm and stood behind her, brushing the soft leather strands over her nipples and shoulder as he did so. "The second it hits you, suck a gasp between your teeth and arch away. If possible, go up on your toes." He pushed her hair over her shoulder. The ends tickled her nipples.

Gaby knew it was for show, that Nick wouldn't hurt her, but that didn't stop her heart from racing or her juices from pooling. They were all nude. She'd have no telltale whisper of clothing tonight to let her know the stroke was coming. In the club, voices and music would also mask the sound. This was a good rehearsal.

"Eyes forward," Reid told her. "Always. Listen. You might think there's no sound, but there is. Seek it."

Gaby closed her eyes and strained her ears. *Yes…there…Nick pulling the strands through his fingers, letting the ends fall as one.* He did it three times. Then the flogger fell over her back. She hissed and arched away.

"Damn," Reid muttered.

She dared a peek at him. His cock was fully charged, rather than semi-awake.

"Good job, sweetheart." Nick tickled the ends over her backside. "After three or four, you can add a moan. I'll be as light as I can. It's up to you to put on a show, distract them with your reaction and that gorgeous body."

"Don't be afraid of hurting me if you have to." Gaby hadn't expected the words to be this difficult to say. She'd taken punches in martial arts, in training, in running down perps. Come home with bruises so bad it was a wonder she hadn't broken something. This was all so different, personal.

Nick stepped to her front and cupped her neck. Fingers massaged the side, thumb traced her jawline. "Too late. All of this makes me more afraid than I can stand."

He kissed her hard, thrusting his tongue deep into her mouth until she melted into his lips. His hard-on nudged her stomach, leaving a trail of pre-cum tattooed on her skin. He jerked away and turned to Reid. Her body chilled at the loss of his heat.

"Let's get this over with," he told Reid.

Reid jerked his head toward the cups he'd prepared. "You're all set. You take the back. I'll take the front. It'll help Gaby and me get better...acquainted."

Nick clenched his jaw and grabbed a cup and paintbrush. He didn't meet Gaby's gaze when he walked behind her. She wanted to reassure him, but didn't have a clue where to start or what to say. She was the one who'd put them on this course. Nick was just seeing she had the skills necessary to carry the job through to a safe conclusion, whether he liked her choice or not. He was letting her do her job, helping her even, despite his reservations. She suspected it might be one of the few times he'd agree. Some part of her was almost sorry he did now. In hindsight, her plan didn't seem the wisest of choices.

Reid finished mixing and started her way. One phrase would stop it all. The evidence folder on the far table kept Gaby from saying it. A murderer on the prowl, and she was seemingly the only hope to find him. Nick would keep her safe. He'd promised. She trusted that.

Cold soft bristles touched her back. Gaby gasped and instinctively pulled away. The movement pushed her breasts in Reid's direction. Reid didn't hesitate. A jerk of his hand slashed a thin, purple line over her nipple. A moan passed her lips. Both men sucked in a breath, yet had the respect to remain otherwise silent.

Gaby closed her eyes and soaked in the sensations. Reid slashed marks over her breasts, stomach, and thighs. Quick, like the whip presumed to have made them. Nick took his time, measuring the strokes he crisscrossed down her back and buttocks. Her breath heaved. Whimpers and moans had a will of their own. Gaby let the pleasure imprint on her memory. She'd draw on that in the hell sure to come when a madman could hold her life in his hands and her only chance of survival was what Nick and Reid gave her now.

Tears swelled behind her eyelids. Fear choked her throat. Distress squeaked out.

"Gaby?" Nick's arm slid around her waist.

"You okay?" Reid cupped her hip.

Gaby wanted to say she was fine. She was a kick-ass cop. She could handle anything. Her chin quivered. Tears slipped down her cheeks. She shook her head.

"No." She shook her head again. "No, and it's not the two of you. It's him. That killer. The thought of him…"

"Shhh." Nick kissed her shoulder. "It's okay, princess. It's okay."

He held her close while Reid released her from the cuffs. The instant she was free, Nick lifted her and carried her to the bed. Reid followed and sat at her feet, massaging them. It helped calm her. Told Gaby everything was going to be all right.

Pulling in a shaky breath, she kissed Nick. He swiped away the tear tracks with his thumbs and nipped at first one lip and then the other. She managed a tremulous smile and nuzzled against him. Reid took that as his sign to leave and pushed away from the bed. He was still hard as a rock. So was Nick.

"No." She reached for Reid, but looked at Nick. "Let's do this one thing. I don't need it to go undercover. I need this for…us."

The want in his eyes snuggled in her heart. He gave Reid a single nod. Everything they needed was in place, except Reid. He hesitated, then finally sat at her feet. Nick snagged condoms from the bedside table and tossed one Reid's way. He caught it in one hand.

"What should I do?" she asked.

Nick smiled. "Nothing except enjoy it."

He plumped the pillows against the headboard, then sat in the nest and pulled Gaby between his legs. When she eased into him, Nick lifted her a little higher and slid his cock deep inside her. His knees kept hers apart and exposed them both to Reid.

"Let him see how pretty you are down there, sweetheart."

Reid's eyes glimmered at the sight. But there was no denying it wasn't just her pussy that got his attention. He raked his gaze from clit to balls.

Gaby sagged into Nick's arms, her lips seeking his as he kneaded long fingers into her breasts. She captured his mouth, lashing her tongue around his, giving and taking, wanting and needing. Her breath caught when Reid's mouth crawled up her leg. Nick twirled her nipples between his fingers, pinching, elongating. She felt every tug spark to her pussy. Gaby clenched tight around his cock, loving the feel of it pulsing inside.

Reid's deep-throated groan wiggled up her thigh. He massaged his thumbs higher and higher, his mouth following in relentless pursuit. Nick raked his hand down to her pussy and parted her folds, inviting Reid to take what he offered. Gaby's juices poured from around Nick's erection and dripped down the crevice until she felt them dampening his pubis. Reid's breath neared, but he moved no farther.

Curious, she broke the kiss. Reid glanced up at her…at them. His gaze never faltered. In seemingly slow motion he dipped low, then licked from the base of Nick's cock to her clit.

Nick groaned and thrust himself deep. Gaby held on and rocked with him. Reid suckled her clit between his lips, then worked back down Nick's cock. Nick thrashed beneath her and grabbed her hips, urging her to fuck him. Reid stilled them both—one hand on Gaby's knee, one on Nick's.

"Take your woman's ass," he ordered. "It's only right that you do."

Nick shifted, hesitated, then slowly eased inside her anus. Gaby grappled for a handhold. Reid caught her hand and laced her fingers through his. Nick clutched her breast. Her nipple burrowed into his palm. She gasped for breath, body shuddering from the pleasure-pain. Her clit cried out for attention, her pussy begged for possession.

Reid knelt between their legs and fisted his cock. Gaby grabbed Nick's free hand and shoved it to her clit. She held her breath, eyes shut, and waited. Three groans hit the ceiling as Reid slid in. They froze, each pulling in gulps of air.

"You have a really tight pussy," Reid whispered. "I'll bet your ass is even tighter."

"It is," Nick replied quickly. "It is."

"Shut up," she gasped. "Just fuck me."

Their chuckles vibrated through her. Gaby writhed on their cocks, demanding they do what she want. Neither moved. They let her take command.

The gift empowered her. Growling, she rocked into them, setting up a rhythm neither could refuse for very long. Nick groaned and countered with a thrust of his own. Reid shook his head, clenched his teeth, and pounded into her. Gaby started to come. Everything tightened. She dug her nails into Nick's hip and Reid's shoulder, determined they reach the peak with her.

"Come with me," she ordered. "Or do I have to use the flogger on both of you?"

They slammed into her and shot. She felt the force through the condoms. She gloried in the power they unleashed and let herself explode. Climatic waves resonated from her core to the tips of her fingers and toes and back again. Gaby didn't realize she'd come back to earth until she lay between them on the bed, their fingers dancing lazy circles up and down her body.

She'd just about drifted off to sleep when the trill of a cell phone snapped her upright. "Shit."

Combing her hair from her face, Gaby stumbled from the bed in search of her jeans. She found them in the far corner of the living room, resting much more comfortably than she was at the moment. Sinking into the chair, she fished the phone from the pocket. Her partner.

"Keating," she answered.

"You're off the hook. Thank fucking God. Stupidest thing I ever..."

"Nestor, don't rant. It's unbecoming. You don't do it to your wife, so don't do it to me. What's going on?"

"They caught the son of a bitch. The fire freak. He walked into police headquarters pretty as you please and turned himself in. Someone had worked his ass and back over good. He could barely sit. Shaking like a leaf. Waived his rights and confessed."

Relief seeped into her muscles. *Thank God.*

She glanced up at Nick in the doorway. Reid was right behind him.

"Good. One less thing we have to worry about. I'll see you in the morning." She disconnected and tossed the phone to the table. "You won't believe it, but that guy turned himself in tonight."

Nick slipped into the car behind her. "The one you wanted to go under to find?"

She wrapped his arms around her waist and snuggled into him. "Yeah. Turned himself in."

Nick shrugged. "Stranger things, I suppose."

"Not really so strange." Reid stepped into his trousers, zipped up, and reached for his shirt. "Gaby, you really don't think your father was actually going to allow you to go undercover to a sex club, do you? If you thought he might, then you really should've known he wasn't serious when he suggested a very high profile rock star and well-known attorney go as your escorts."

She sat upright. "He did this? How?"

Reid shrugged. "Can't say. I was here with you." He snagged his shoes and gave them a wink. "Get some sleep. You both could use it. As for me…I've had enough surprises for one night. Maybe I'll go find a few of my own instead of sharing everyone else's."

Dumbstruck, Gaby watched him leave. "What just happened here?"

Nick pulled her against him and kissed her neck. "Oh…I'm thinking magic."

She snuggled deep. "I'm thinking you just might be right."

EPILOGUE

And then there were none.

In an announcement that broke hearts around the world, we learned Nick Tristan married Gabrielle Keating in a private ceremony this weekend in Palm Springs. This one came out of the blue. But that seems to be the norm lately with Mesquite. When fans around the world were reeling over the news that Brian Tristan was married with a child, Paul Tristan was engaged to Ceci Powers, and the love-hate relationship between Caz Tristan and Brooke Hansen was definitely love, this little tidbit snuck in under our radar.

Who is the blushing bride? Former police officer and daughter of Mesquite attorney Marvin Keating. So apparently Nick and Gaby have known each other for a while. Proud father Marvin gave his daughter away during the ceremony at Diversions Resort. Family and close friends attended. When asked what's next for our sneaky couple, Nick says, "Maybe we'll find a quiet cabin somewhere for a little vacation. Who knows? Maybe I'll write a book and we'll fill up our house with a bunch of kids."

Speaking of offspring...

Finally, the news we've been on the edge of our seats waiting for. Yes, Paul and Ceci are pregnant! With, of course, twins! "Isn't that what all celebrity couples do?" Paul told us. Apparently not, since Brian and Lexy have a little one on the way as well.

So, how is Ceci going to find the time when she's busy organizing the new Tristan Foundation? It won't be with Brooke's help. She's helping Mesquite form their own production company and record label. And, Lexy, the woman whose presence started the dominoes of single-hood falling for our handsome brothers? She coyly reports she's quietly content, but we have it on good authority she's started her own interior design company.

Whatever Mesquite does, we're sure to be thoroughly enthralled and entertained by them...and their four little heartbreakers.

Caitlyn Willows

Erotic romance author Caitlyn Willows weaves deep emotions and sizzling sensuality into her action-filled stories. Believing life is to be lived and felt, not merely watched, Willows delivers real-to-life characters in unforgettable tales of love, adventure, and always steamy passion.

Caitlyn Willows's email address is caitlyn@caitlynwillows.com.

2296976

Made in the USA